Voices. Had he heard voices?

Sure enough, in the distance Trent spotted the three gunmen climbing up the trail. His pulse raced.

Any noise at this point could alert them to movement inside the cabin. "Come," he ordered his K-9, Rex. He tiptoed to Brooke's side and touched her shoulder.

"Brooke, wake up." Her eyes popped open. He put a finger to his lips. "Shhh, they're back and headed this way. Implement plan B."

She gasped and stared at him, wide-eyed. "What's plan B?"

"Out the back door and hide. Be quiet." He rushed to the window. Goose bumps crawled up his spine. He could throw a rock and hit them. They were close. Too close.

He hooked the leash on Rex's collar. The dog growled. "I know. Quiet. I'll let you know if I need your assistance."

Brooke slid to her feet, holding her belly. Poor Brooke. Just when she should be eagerly anticipating the arrival of her newborn, she was running for her life...and the life of her baby.

Loretta Eidson is an award-winning author born and raised in the South. She lives with her husband, Kenneth, in North Mississippi and enjoys family time with her four children and thirteen grandchildren. Her love of reading began at a young age when she discovered Phyllis Whitney's mystery novels. Loretta believes in the power of prayer and loves putting her characters in situations where they must trust God to pull them through. Visit Loretta on her website at lorettaeidson.com.

Pursued in the Wilderness

LORETTA EIDSON

LOVE INSPIRED
INSPIRATIONAL ROMANCE

LOVE INSPIRED®
INSPIRATIONAL ROMANCE

ISBN-13: 978-1-335-42618-5

Pursued in the Wilderness

Recycling programs
for this product may
not exist in your area.

For questions and comments about the quality of this book, please contact us at CustomerService@Harlequin.com.

Love Inspired
22 Adelaide St. West, 41st Floor
Toronto, Ontario M5H 4E3, Canada
www.LoveInspired.com

Printed in U.S.A.

Fear thou not; for I am with thee: be not dismayed;
for I am thy God: I will strengthen thee;
yea, I will help thee; yea, I will uphold thee
with the right hand of my righteousness.
—*Isaiah* 41:10

This book is dedicated to my husband, Kenneth,
and family and friends for cheering me on
and my beta readers, Monnie, Cheryl and Edwina.
Special thanks to the Suspense Squad.

Acknowledgments

I want to acknowledge my friend Mario Alberti,
(retired) sergeant, Tampa Police Department K-9,
and (retired) acting branch chief, DHS TSA National
Explosives Detection Canine Training Program
(NEDCTP), for his wisdom, insight and direction
as I wrote this book. I extend a memorial to his K-9,
Rex 1, who served his handler well.

I extend a special appreciation
for my editor, Adrienne Macintosh,
and my agent, Tamela Hancock Murray.
You are all a godsend.

Chapter One

"What is it this time, Nick?" Brooke Chandler looked at her cell and rolled her eyes.

"It's important. I need to see you immediately," he said. "Texted my location. A remote cabin in Chilhowee Mountain. Need you to meet me tonight. It's urgent. And don't tell anyone where I am."

"You can't be serious. You know how I feel about the wilderness."

"This one time. I won't ever ask you again."

Her stomach plummeted. She had avoided the mountains for years. Bears were vicious, and she wanted no part of them. His insistence got the best of her.

"Fine, but you know at thirty-eight weeks, I shouldn't be going anywhere except to the hospital. If I drive all the way out there, you're signing the divorce papers."

"Make sure no one follows you." His self-inflicted drama infuriated her.

All her countless arguments met with closed ears. Three happy years of marriage drowned out by four grueling years of coping with his addiction that only grew worse. He'd left her with no other choice. She had to put an end to the turmoil before it affected their baby.

With divorce papers in hand, Brooke scooped her car keys and purse off the counter and stormed out the door. She slid into the car, sent a text to her mom and slammed her hand against the steering wheel, scolding herself for giving in.

Her pulse increased the closer she got to the foothills. The bear attack she'd witnessed eighteen years ago flashed in her mind. If she'd backed away from that cub, the mother wouldn't have attacked the man who tried to protect her. No doubt, it was all her fault. Her knuckles whitened the tighter she squeezed the steering wheel. Hair on her arms lifted. The man lived, but still, she'd caused his pain. She hadn't been in the woods since the incident and had avoided animals altogether, wild or domestic.

Her car's GPS led her along a mountain road. She maneuvered the winding curves where the road grew narrower. The asphalt changed to gravel, and the sun faded behind the trees. Her insides churned. Nick's truck sat at the edge of a pitted gravel driveway. She pulled in beside it and parked.

The ramshackle cabin teetered at the edge of a ravine and looked ready to collapse. Half of the wooden front porch had rotted and caved in. The screen door dangled on one hinge and missing shingles left the rafters exposed. Dust and cobwebs clouded the windows. How had he found this place? The sooner he signed the papers, the better.

She eased onto the unstable porch. He opened the rickety wood door, yanked her inside and slammed it behind her. The floor creaked with each step. Would it support her weight?

She shoved the papers at him. "Sign these and tell me what's so important."

"I screwed up and lost a bet." He paced and wiped his brow. "They're looking for me. They want their money."

"What does that have to do with me, Nick? That's your problem." She thrust the pen at him. "How many times have I begged you to get help for your gambling addiction? Face your losses and give them what you owe."

"Can't. I'm broke. And now they're coming after our baby before he's even born. Said they'd sell him on the black market as payment for what I owe."

"Don't threaten me like that." Her mouth went dry. "Sign the papers and I'm done." Her hand smoothed over her belly and patted gently. No one would take her baby. She dropped her purse and keys on the small wooden table and marched into the kitchen, where a case of bottled water sat on the dusty kitchen counter. She gripped the edge of the countertop. He couldn't be serious, could he?

She stared into the forest from the cracked kitchen window. A large wasp nest had her backing away. The threat of nightfall gripped her, and an ache hit her low back. She'd stop at the hotel about fifteen minutes away and make the drive home early in the morning.

A sudden thud and the crackling of boards breaking startled her. A rush of stomping footsteps sent her pulse racing into overtime. She spun. A bearded man jerked Nick up by the collar and pressed a gun to his head. Another man clomped around him, holding a handgun in the air. A third man stood out of sight, but the tips of his brown boots came into view.

"Where is she?" A gruff voice permeated the cabin.

"No. Don't. I'll get the money." Panic rose in Nick's response. His eyes cut toward her. "Brooke! Run!"

The water bottle slipped from her hand. She darted out the back door, searching for a place to hide.

Her heartbeat thrashed in her ears. Who were they? She stumbled forward and almost fell. Her breath caught in her chest. She grabbed the moss-covered trunk of a large tree just outside the back door and slipped behind it. Her arms wrapped around her protruding belly as she gasped for breath. Her legs shook.

Nick's words reverberated in her ears. "They want our baby." She'd half listened and hadn't taken him seriously. What had he gotten them into?

She peeked around the tree, and her hand scraped across the brittle wooden corner of the cabin. The forest terrified her. She bit her lip. Should she keep running? Had they seen her flee? After Nick yelled her name and told her to run, they had to have known she was there. He had manipulated and lied too many times. She couldn't trust anyone but herself.

Brooke peered into the depths of the forest. Where were the bears, coyotes and all the other wild animals? Her muscles tensed. She couldn't do this. She never wanted to return to the mountains. Not now. Not ever. But she had. Big mistake.

Something crashed to the floor inside the cabin. She jumped back and hugged the tree. A loud thud. Shuffling feet, and the sound of a scuffle. Her imagination went wild. Were they beating Nick and slamming him against the walls? Angry male voices seeped beyond the thickness of the log structure as Nick begged for his life.

"No, don't, please. I'll get your money." Nick's voice escalated to a high pitch.

The bang of gunfire invaded her ears. Silence.

Her legs caved, and she sank to the ground. She covered her mouth with both hands and smothered the terror-filled scream spilling from her lips. Tears rolled like a tsunami. Had they killed him? Was she next? Would they kill her and her baby? No. According to Nick, they *wanted* her baby. Panic shot adrenaline through her like an electrical charge, and she sprang to her feet. She couldn't let them find her.

Brooke wiped tears and blinked. The evening sun dipped lower below the horizon, thrusting her into darkness. A coyote howled and branches rustled. How could she survive out here alone?

The men stepped out the back door.

"Zeke. Told you not to kill Nick until we had the girl," a gruff voice growled. "Lose her and we lose the cash. You get trigger-happy again and you're done."

She sucked in a gulp of air. Nick. Dead? That wasn't the out she'd wanted. She'd loved and trusted him. He'd been a good husband, managed their finances and made wise decisions for their future, until the last four years. Their savings dwindled to nothing, her diamond jewelry disappeared and his work ethics spiraled. She thought he was her forever soul mate, but his actions proved her mistaken. How could she have trusted him implicitly? She'd been so wrong.

Grief consumed her. They *were* after her baby. Nick had told the truth. If only it were another one of his lies.

Images of what could happen to her and Josiah flashed through her mind. Lamaze class taught breathing techniques to use during labor. Would it help keep her from hyperventilating or passing out?

"She won't get far in her condition." The man's gravelly voice carried into the quiet forest. He coughed and spat. "Let's grab flashlights from the truck." They tromped back inside.

"Can't risk losing her," she heard one of them shout from the front of the cabin. A vehicle door slammed. "That kid is our ticket out of here." There was something familiar about his voice, but she couldn't place it.

She bolted deeper into the thick forest. Each slap of spindly branches felt like arms preventing her escape. She fought her way through them. Her insides trembled uncontrollably.

Had they followed her to the cabin, or were they hiding? Waiting for her arrival? Maybe they didn't know she and Nick had been separated.

Mosquitos buzzed around her ears. Didn't matter. She kept running. Her feet stumbled on the uneven ground and leaves slapped her face. The baby kicked her side. *I know, Josiah. I know. Oh God, please help me.*

Sweat from the mid-August heat soaked her short-sleeved top and rolled down her back. Her capris and sockless sneakers left half her calves exposed. Weeds slashed against her ankles. A quick glance back. Three flashlights shone in the distance, moving slower than she expected. Maybe they assumed she couldn't run. A dull ache hit her abdomen.

Don't go into labor out here. She paused and took a few quick breaths. The pain eased, and she pushed deeper into the inky darkness. Flashes of Nick's pacing and warning before he died overshadowed her vision. He'd apologized profusely before their separation and admitted he'd made a lot of poor decisions. But he didn't stop gambling and never admitted he had an addiction.

She stumbled to her knees. Heavy sobs sucked the breath out of her as her fists punched the ground. Nausea threatened. She hadn't wanted him to die, but how could he not know something horrible would happen?

She wiped her eyes with the hem of her blouse and pushed to her feet. With outstretched arms, she felt her way deeper into the woods, making sure each foot landed on level ground. Something pierced her palm. *Ouch!* A thorn, probably. "Please don't let it be a black widow, brown recluse, fire ant or whatever else is out here. I can't stop now," she huffed breathlessly.

Her pulse pounded hard. The mountains were bad enough in daylight, but nighttime heightened eerie sounds. Frogs croaked, crickets chirped and birds chattered. Were they frightened, too? Calling out for help? Another howl from the distance sent weakness down her legs. The constant reminders of wild animals ran loose. Bears, coyotes, wild hogs, bobcats, wolves, snakes. She flinched at every sound.

An unnerving silence fell over the forest. Her knees almost buckled again. Where were the killers? Tiny dots of light from their flashlights shone in the distance. They'd misjudged the adrenaline surge that pushed her forward.

Brooke gulped down another breath. A light breeze blew and chilled her sweaty body. The sound of leaves tossing in the wind eased her somehow. Smoke. A fire?

She squinted in the darkness. There in the distance a light flickered. Hope of survival thrust away overpowering fear. She forced herself to keep moving, one step at a time, being sure-footed. Closer and closer.

How far had she run? Another glance back. Total blackness. Her belly tightened and pulled her to an abrupt halt. She wrapped her arms around her tummy, and focused on breathing. Braxton-Hicks contractions or the real thing? Her instructor warned her these could occur, but would the trauma of her situation and all the running thrust her into labor? *Please, no.* Weakness consumed her. She fought against dropping to the ground again.

"If I ever make it home, I'll never come here again," she whispered. "And I'll never trust anyone again, especially myself."

K-9 handler Trent Williston shot up from a deep sleep. His heart raced while vivid sounds of sirens wailing, his own labored breathing as he did CPR, the sight and smell of blood and a woman crying bombarded his thoughts and turned his stomach.

He blinked and looked around, swallowing hard. Must have fallen asleep watching the flames dance in the fire. Another guilt-ridden nightmare. When would they stop?

Rex, his black-and-tan German shepherd, jumped to his feet and barked at Trent's sudden movement. He stood and whined, wagging his tail.

Trent rolled to his feet.

Rex pushed his nose under Trent's hand. Trent leaned and buried his face in the dog's thick fur. The canine's woodsy scent proved they were still in the Smoky Mountains.

"We had a good workout today. Good boy, you did great."

Rex nuzzled Trent's neck and licked him.

"I love you, too." Trent stretched his arms to the sky, lowered them and rolled his shoulders. Leaves rustled in the trees with the evening breeze. Smoldering smoke from his campfire assaulted his nose.

Rex roamed the perimeter of the camp, stopping occasionally to mark his territory. Trent paced and listened to the whippoorwills sing their evening song in an attempt to get the nightmare out of his mind.

"Can't believe we've been here five days already. Only two more days of bliss, boy, before we pack up and head home. We've got some big decisions to make. Stay with the K-9 unit, move to the training center or transfer somewhere where there are no risks? One thing's for sure, I won't renew my EMT license. That should put a halt to delivering another baby."

Rex jumped and rested his front paws on Trent's thighs. Trent smirked and petted his fur before pushing him away.

"God was supposed to help in times of trouble. Right, Rex?"

His tactical watch vibrated on his arm. Six twenty p.m. was his normal evening jogging time, but nothing was normal about this camping trip. Too much weighed on his mind and had him distracted. Not a good thing when his job required his full attention. He sucked in a deep breath and blew it out with a huff. Taking a sudden vacation wasn't like him. But Sergeant Owens had insisted on a few days off to pull himself together. Who was he to argue?

"Time to liven up the fire." He glanced at Rex. "I don't know about you, buddy, but I need a cup of coffee, a can of sausages and a good night's sleep. Three weeks of restlessness is getting the best of me."

Rex gave a short yelp and stepped back.

"Guess you'd like fresh water in your bowl and some food. If you behave, I'll add a drop or two of my coffee."

Rex trotted over to his empty bowl and looked back.

"You're too smart for your own good." Trent poured half a bottle of water into the bowl and the rest over his head. He shook the water from his hair, then combed it back with his fingers and scratched at his stubbled chin. "Should've brought my razor. This stuff itches."

His mind scrolled through all the supplies he'd packed for this seven-day camping trip away from work, friends and, well, pregnant women. Just him and Rex. No special deliveries. He'd estimated just right. Enough food to get them by for the next two days. Not bad for an unplanned escape to the mountains.

A whiff of coffee brought a deep sniff. Trent slid on a glove and grabbed the metal coffeepot off the fire. He poured the liquid energy into his metal cup, sat on the log and took a big gulp. "Whoa, that's hot. Probably not a good idea if I'm wanting to sleep."

Rex eased over and plopped on the ground beside him.

He put a bite of mini sausage in his mouth and pulled his cell from his pocket. "Want to listen to Mandy's message again? No signal out here, but we can still hear her sweet voice."

Rex whined.

Trent selected the message his sister, Dana, sent the day he arrived at the ranger's station and put it on Speaker.

"Hey, little brother, you must be busy or out of cell range since you didn't answer my call. You haven't been yourself lately and I'm concerned. I don't like you going camping alone, and I don't care how experienced you are, it's just not safe. Anyway, thanks for stopping by before your trip. Mandy gets a kick out of hiding surprises in your backpack."

His niece's dainty voice sounded in the background. Trent adored her and imagined her jumping into his arms with those long curls bouncing against her shoulders. Listening to her talk warmed his heart. Someday he'd have a family of his own.

"I wanna talk, please, let me talk."

"Mandy wanted to talk to you. That's why I'm calling," Dana said.

"Hi, Uncle Trent. Did you find your surprise? Are you coming to my birthday party? Can Rex come, too? You put a whole muffin in your mouth." She giggled. "You're funny. Mama won't let me do that. I want a baby doll with a puppy for my birthday. Are you coming?"

Dana took the phone. "Seriously, Trent. Be careful. Call us if you need anything. Love you."

He clicked off the message and dropped the phone back into his pocket. "You know what that means, don't you, Rex? We've got to find a doll with a puppy if they make one like that." He paused and pointed at his canine. "Don't let me forget her party next week. Turning five is a big deal and we'll be in big trouble if we're not back to eat cake and ice cream with her. Besides, I promised I'd be there."

Trent finished off the sausages and took another sip of his coffee. He set his cup on the log. He traipsed into the tent for his night goggles, grabbed a nutrition bar from the backpack, along with a meal pack for Rex, and his Do Not Pet K-9 vest. The goggles had proven an asset while doing night training exercises in the woods with Rex. He slid them over his head.

Rex danced around him and barked.

"I know, I'd rather head straight home when we leave here, too, but I'm a man of my word." He grabbed his coffee and emptied the cup. "Well, maybe not." He swiped his hand across his lips. The image of a pregnant lady tossed from her mangled car out on the interstate flashed through his mind. *Stop.* His knuckles whitened in his fist. Would he ever be able to get that image and the events of that night out of his mind?

Trent sat by the fire reminiscing the past few days. Trekking seven miles over the level-nine hiking trail four days ago held its challenges, but he loved the scenic views of mountains peeking through the clouds and stretching across the sky as far as he could see. The enormous rock formations and ravines below. Trees, vines, wildflowers and ferns everywhere. Not to mention the occasional glimpse of a bear or deer in the distance.

Conquering steep inclines along the trail enhanced his opinion of a successful climb. Today was no different. The exercise helped strengthen his muscles and keep his mind off his dilemma. The whole reason for this trip, getting a grip on his emotions and the hollow feeling in his gut.

The days had flown by. He wiped sweat from his forehead. Rex munched on his beefy food and lapped his water from the bowl Trent had packed in the backpack. A twelve-point buck sprang from his bed one day and bounced light-footedly deeper into the forest. Such a majestic sight.

He stared into the woods. How could anyone deny God's existence with all the beauty around him? And yet, where was God when he needed him most? Rex barked, drawing him back to reality. "I know, I know." He packed up their trash, stuffed it into a trash bag, placed it in the tent and began reorganizing the supplies in his backpack.

Mandy's surprise package fell out. He'd looked at it earlier in the week. What did she think he'd do with a small doll holding a baby bottle, wrapped in a soft blue blanket that swallowed her? He shook his head and smiled at Mandy's innocence. Just glad none of his coworkers were there to rag him about having a doll. With everything stored back in place, he set the backpack inside his tent.

Rex trotted toward him. Trent took the vest off his dog and set it on a log. He put the leash on him and walked through heeling techniques and verbal markers. Rex aced them all. He never ceased to amaze Trent with his intelligence and prompt obedience. His faithful friend for life. He unhooked Rex's leash and tossed it aside. He sprayed his arms and neck with mosquito spray before gathering more limbs for the fire.

Within a few minutes, the fire crackled again, and

flames danced. Darkness surrounded the camp. A coyote howled in the distance adding to the ambiance of the forest. His two-person tent sat empty. If he only had someone special to share the joys of nature, and everything he loved about the mountains.

"Peace, at last." He threw his arm over Rex and rubbed his fur. His thoughts drifted back to the wreck and his part of the rescue that went all wrong. His partner said the preemie's death wasn't his fault, but he blamed himself. He was search and rescue and should've been better prepared. Sorrow stirred in his gut.

Only two more days and he'd have to choose the direction of his career. Indecision gnawed at him. Trent kicked back by the fire and looked up. The stars twinkled as the stillness of the night settled in. Thankfully, there were no pregnant women to deal with in the woods.

Rex lay at his side. He reached down and tossed the fur on his canine's head and sighed. Rex jumped to his feet, faced the woods, and let out a low growl. Trent followed his canine's lead and stands, searching to see what Rex had heard.

Chapter Two

The intense pain eased in Brooke's abdomen. She bolted upright and floundered through the tall grass. Her sneakers wet and heavy with mud. The woodsy scent of a campfire assaulted her nose. A scent she loved as a child. Her eyes strained to see who was at the camp. Something furry stood and faced her direction. A bear? Couldn't be. A man stood looking her direction. She hesitated, took in a shaky breath and drew closer. Her pulse pounded in her ears.

No, it was a big dog, a German shepherd. Her chin and lips trembled. A twig snapped under her foot. The dog barked and stepped forward. The man took a step forward. Something like binoculars hung around his neck. He drew a pistol. Would he shoot her? Would the dog attack?

The man put his hand down and said something. The dog stopped barking, but his growling continued. Her muscles tensed. She imagined his sharp teeth cutting into her leg. Did the man belong with the thugs who were after her? Was anyone hidden in the tent?

She stumbled. Her hands slapped the damp, leafy ground. She caught herself, pushed to her feet and lurched forward. More sobs erupted as she emerged from the darkness into the light of his camp.

The dog danced in place, growling and barking.

"Quiet," the man said, and the shepherd obeyed.

"Please don't shoot. Th…they killed my husband, uh, almost-ex-husband. They're after me."

He clipped his gun back at his waist and ran to her with the dog by his side. Growls pierced her ears.

"What are you talking about? What are you doing out here alone?" He helped her to the log where a small black vest with large white letters that read Do Not Pet, Chattanooga Police K-9 Unit was draped. A leash lay on the ground.

His gentle grip on her arm consoled her. Police. He would help her, but the dog hadn't convinced her.

She eased down on the hard surface, pushed long hair from her sweaty face and pressed her hand against her chest. The dog looked at the man, then back at her. He inched forward and sniffed her feet.

"Don't try petting him. He's checking you out. As long as you do what I say, he won't bother you."

"No worries there. I won't." She leaned away from the furry creature and froze. He sniffed her abdomen, then sat with his back straight and ears up.

"Can you make him go away?" Her voice quivered. "I don't like animals."

"He can sense your fear. Rex. Come here, boy." Trent eases the dog away. "She doesn't want you too close." He petted the dog's long fur and looked at her. "What are you doing out here in your condition?"

"Running for my life. You've got to help me. Three men busted into the cabin and killed him. I… I ran out the back door. Now, they're after me. They have flashlights." She wrung her hands.

Light from the fire flickered in the man's eyes. His eyebrows lowered. Did he believe her? His black T-shirt read Chattanooga Police K-9 Unit. She'd seen similar ones on police officers who frequented her bakery. Her body shivered. He could protect her, but his dog had to go.

"What did you mean, almost-ex-husband? Here, have some water." He handed her a bottle and kept one for himself. "It's an unbelievable story. How do I know you didn't kill your 'almost-ex-husband' and you're running from authorities?"

She buried her face in her hands. "Should've known you wouldn't believe me. A pregnant lady darting through the woods after dark. I wouldn't believe it myself, but here I am, running for my life in the worst imaginable place possible."

"Start from the beginning. Who killed who, and if he was your *almost*-ex-husband, why were you there?"

Brooke dropped her hands. "I don't know who killed him. He begged me to meet him and told me to make sure no one followed. Said he had something important to tell me. I drove to the cabin just so he couldn't make any more excuses for not signing our divorce papers." She looked behind her for signs of the men.

"That drive is over two hours. Were you spending the night?"

"No way. He chose gambling over our marriage. Signing those papers should've only taken a minute. I planned to stay at the hotel, just fifteen minutes away, before heading home in the morning."

A deep, guttural growl sounded. Rex stood and faced the woods.

"Is he going to bite me?" Her heart jumped into her throat.

"Not unless I give the order. He hears something in the woods."

She stood. Why hadn't he tied the dog up or something? Rex turned toward her and growled.

"Rex, sit." The man lowered his eyebrows.

Brooke hinged on hyperventilation. She couldn't just stand there with this monstrous dog ready to pounce. The drumroll in her chest had her senses on high alert.

"You...you don't understand. These men are looking for me right now. They killed him. I... I can't stay here. Look, now you can see their flashlights flickering in the woods." She eased toward the edge of his camp. "I've got to go."

Rex barked. His growl unnerved her. The hair on her arms lifted.

"Wait. Say I believe you. It's treacherous out there, especially after dark. You'll never make it by yourself. I know the trail to the ranger's station. Let me grab my backpack." He turned to his dog. "Stay."

She stilled and chewed her lip, trying to ignore the canine's stare. Finding a police officer in the middle of the forest encouraged her and gave her a measure of peace, but trepidation over his menacing-looking K-9 frightened her. Could she trust this stranger with her life? With Josiah's life? Police officers are trustworthy, right? But, why was he out here alone? She didn't trust herself. Best keep an eye on him and maintain a safe distance from Rex. At least, she wouldn't be alone if a bear came after her.

"Do you have a phone? I ran from the cabin so fast that I left everything behind. My purse, my phone, my house keys. Everything. Glad I had my tennis shoes on." She picked at her fingernail. "I need to call my parents and let them know what's happened. They'll call for help."

"Busted my satellite phone when I tossed this backpack over my head two days ago. It flew out of my hand and hit a rock. My cell is in the pocket of my backpack, but the mountain blocks the nearest cell tower, so the signal won't pick up until we're over the top."

The man grabbed his dog's vest and leash, then rushed inside the tent. He reappeared with a backpack on his back and clipped the leash to Rex's collar. He kicked dirt over the fire, smothering the flames. Darkness fell over the camp.

"This way." His tone grew urgent.

"What about your tent?"

"Forget it—the men carrying those lights are getting closer."

She looked behind her. Three flashlights spread evenly apart had gained ground. An urgency shot through her. She spun and followed him into the dark forest as best she could. Her foot slipped, and she almost turned her ankle. "I can't see."

His warm hand touched her arm and slid down to her hand. "Here, hang on and stay with me. I'm Trent Williston, by the way. K-9 handler with the Chattanooga

Police Department. I suppose you've figured that out already."

She was uncertain about holding this tall, muscular stranger's hand. His unkempt dark hair and scruffy beard gave him a rugged appearance. His long fingers wrapped around hers and held firm. Had she made a wise decision to traipse off into the unknown with him?

"Yes. I did, and I'm glad to find you out here. I'm Brooke Chandler. I own a bakery in Chattanooga. Thank you for helping me." Her insides trembled. The horrifying sound of Nick's screams and the thud of gunshots rang in her ears. This whole mess was all his fault. Guilt choked her for blaming him, but it was the truth. Those men were here because of him. He'd already paid the ultimate price, but she wasn't about to give them her baby.

"Like I said, there are three of them. Best I could tell, two are tall and thin, and have beards and guns. I'm not sure about the third one," she whispered. "But he was wearing cowboy boots." She held her free hand out in front of her, hoping to avoid branches slapping her face again.

"Have you seen them before?" He paused and helped her over a stump.

"No. Thought I recognized one man's voice when he yelled the name Zeke, but I can't recall where I've heard it." She took in a quick breath and jerked her hand from his. A hard ache crept up her belly. She moaned and leaned forward, holding her abdomen.

Trent's hand touched her shoulder. "Are you in labor?"

She exhaled slowly as the pain faded. "I don't know.

My Lamaze instructor said I could have false labor pains called Braxton-Hicks, but I'm afraid it could be the real thing after all that's happened tonight."

"Heard about those. Studied them in EMT class." He found her hand again. "Don't worry. Rex and I will protect you. You ready? Need to keep moving. Wouldn't want to deliver a baby on the run. Problem is, I parked my truck at the ranger's station seven miles away. I love hiking in the Smoky Mountains. You came from the direction of the Chilhowee Mountains. They merge with the Smokies. I hiked all this way to find the perfect spot to set up camp."

Seven miles? Could she make it that far?

He slowed his pace. "Watch your step—it's uneven." He held her arm and helped her over a rutted place.

"Shouldn't your cell battery be dead by now? How can you see?" Something buzzed around her head. She swatted the air there with her free hand, then wiped her face. The salty perspiration burned her palm, reminding her of the thorn puncture.

"I'm wearing night goggles. They help increase vision in the dark." He chuckled. "Special ordered them for night training with Rex. Thought it would be fun to test them while I was out here relaxing. And I recharge my cell with portable power banks."

Smart guy. He seemed to love nature, hanging out in the wild and hiking. All the activities she'd given up a long time ago, including a pet. She preferred admiring the mountains from the window of her cozy home in Chattanooga.

"Makes me feel a little better knowing you can see what's going on around us. Can you spot a bear if it is close to us? The silence is eerie." Her sense of hearing had intensified after those men kicked in the cabin door. "At other times, the slightest noise makes my imagination go haywire."

"Only in the direction I'm looking, so keep your ears open."

"Can you still see the flashlights?" She startled when something snapped off to the side. Had the thugs caught up with them?

A pregnant lady had fallen into his camp, gasping for breath, dirty from head to toe and frantic. Striking him at his shoulder, her small frame had him towering over her. Strands of tangled light brown hair hung in her tear streaked, frightened face. She must have witnessed her husband's murder and ran for her life. His stomach plummeted. Her story sounded like something out of a horror movie. He hadn't wanted to get involved, but how could he not, he *was* a cop. The fear in her eyes convinced him she told the truth. Especially when the lights grew closer to his camp.

Rex growled and lunged forward. His ears stood straight.

"Quiet." He tugged the leash, and Rex stilled. He loved his canine. They were an inseparable team and had been for over five years. Rex could smell the hormonal change in her pregnant body. He was a trained search and rescue dog, but who knew he would allow her into his personal space?

Trent threw his arm out. Brooke halted.

"Oh, it's just a deer." The animal bounced through the woods with its white tail standing tall.

"My heart is in my throat. I'm not much of an out-doorsy person."

"Not everyone loves the outdoors." Didn't take much to figure out she was a city girl. Recoiling from Rex was understandable. Hoots of a horned owl and the high-pitched whistles of an elk frightened her.

He slowed and looked behind them. Adrenaline shot through his veins. The flashlights had gained ground and were closer than he expected. If they found his camp, they'd suspect she had help. The hair on the back of his neck bristled.

He mentally kicked himself for leaving his police gear and handcuffs in the glove compartment of his truck. At least, he'd packed his pistol and big game gun. He and Rex could take on the three suspects, but traipsing seven miles over winding trails and multiple inclines through the mountain range with them in tow while protecting a pregnant lady wasn't safe.

"You see them, don't you?" Her voice shook.

"Yep. We can't outrun them." Trent's heart pounded in his ears. Rex growled again. "Quiet." He fell silent, and his dark eyes stared up at him. "Good, boy." Trent patted him on the head.

Her hand shook inside his. What was this trauma doing to her baby?

"We're not on the main hiking trail yet. It's up ahead. They'll expect us to follow it back to the station. Rex and I could take them on, but it wouldn't be safe for you. We're going to hide and let them pass us."

Sniffles met his ears. He couldn't bear hearing a lady cry, especially a pregnant one. Not much he could do to console her at this point.

"I can't lose Josiah," she whispered.

"Who?"

"My baby. I'm naming him after my grandfather, Reginald Josiah. You two would've hit it off. He enjoyed camping, too."

"We're not losing anyone. Rex and I will keep you safe." And he would, but delivering a baby wasn't in the plan.

"Where do we hide? Aren't there coyotes out here, too? And snakes, spiders and…and all those poisonous bugs? Won't that hurt Josiah?"

The fear in her voice made him more determined to get her out of harm's way and back home. He tugged her off in another direction. Snakes, bugs and spiders were part of the wilderness, like bears and coyotes. She'd have to deal with it. "I'll find us a place. Stay with me." He couldn't guarantee she wouldn't encounter any wildlife.

"With you is the only place I can be right now." She tripped.

He caught her before she hit the ground. "Careful. There's a big brush pile over to the left. Let's check it out."

He unclipped his pistol and held it in front of him as they drew closer to the thicket. Extending the leash allowed Rex to scout the area out ahead of them.

Rex wagged his tail, sniffed, looked back, then proceeded around the bend. If Trent were a praying man, he'd pray they weren't infringing on a bear's bed, but he wasn't so he had to depend on his canine's reactions, and his own intuition and knowledge. The sound of rushing water drew closer. *Perfect. A stream. Rex can get a drink.*

Trent evaluated the location of the fallen trees and brush. If he took her around the top end of the thicket, the guys wouldn't notice since they were tracking from the south. Confidence in his assessment of the men kept him moving toward the hideout. Unexperienced hikers like them didn't mean they weren't dangerous but carrying a weapon with intent to kill was against the law.

"Can you identify these guys? Any idea who the others are? You said one of them is Zeke. Do you know why they killed your husband?"

"I don't know who they are, or how they knew where to find us, unless they followed Nick or followed me. I'm in the dark, like you. No pun intended." Her voice cracked. He deserved an explanation now that he'd put his life on the line for her. "But I know why they're after me."

"Yeah, why's that?" She had his attention.

"They want my baby as payment for Nick's gambling debt. He said they were dangerous men, and they planned to sell Josiah on the black market to get their money."

Heat rushed to Trent's face. How absurd. No way would he let that happen. Now he understood her desperation. All this horror should have thrown her into labor, still could, or may have already.

"Not going to happen. I'm getting you out of here."

He clipped this weapon back onto his belt and pulled her around the tall grass and fallen tree. Several large rocks protruded from the ground, along with entangled tree roots. He stepped closer, holding her sides so she didn't trip. The baby kicked his hand. His heart squeezed. *Amazing. And yet, a grim reminder of his situation with a pregnant lady and the possibility of another emergency delivery.*

No signs of animals. Bugs, probably.

"Watch your step." He let go of her full waistline and held her arm. "There's a rock in front of you. Turn around and sit. When they get closer, we'll have to get on the ground." He slid his backpack off and placed it up under the trees. "Come, Rex. Sit."

The dog promptly curled up on the ground at Brooke's feet. He sniffed her legs. She held her hands up and turned her head like she expected an attack.

"I'll do anything to keep them from finding me." She groaned. "Having another contraction." Her slow, deep breathing was consistent with the EMT classes he'd taken.

"Is this your first? How far along are you?"

"Yes, my first. I'm thirty-eight weeks as of a couple of days ago." She blew out a long breath.

"Doctors normally frown on women traveling when they reach their third trimester." He studied her through his goggles. She rubbed her face with both hands. The swelling around her eyes still prominent from crying.

"True. But I didn't think driving to the cabin and going right back home would be a big deal. I argued with Nick about it, but you see who won. He destroyed my love for him with his lying, gambling and manipulative ways. I figured the sooner he signed the divorce papers, the sooner I could get on with my life."

He raised up and scanned the forest. A couple more minutes and they'd need to crouch closer to the ground.

He checked the whereabouts of the men. "Get down. They're getting closer." Rex stood and growled in a low tone. "Shh, quiet." He patted the canine's side. The three thugs tromped up the trail with their low-powered flashlights and hadn't spread out. Obviously, they were unprepared to search the wilderness.

Trent helped Brooke sit on the ground. She leaned against the big rock while he sat in front of her where he could monitor their location. "Sound travels, so stay quiet and don't move."

Rex shifted his stance and held his head high. Trent observed his dog's apprehension of her. Despite her fear, his partner sensed she was in a vulnerable state. The shepherd watched Trent's reactions toward her for confirmation of acceptance. Such a smart, loyal canine.

Her eyes widened. She wiped her hand across the hard surface and rested her head on the rock. Mosquitos buzzed around her, but she didn't twitch. How terrified and miserable she must be. His pulse raced and pounded in his ears. One hand rested on the pistol clipped to his belt. He didn't want to shoot anyone, but he wouldn't let anyone harm her.

The men stopped on the trail. Rex stood with his ears lifted. Trent patted him and rubbed his head. He put his finger to his lips.

Rex stared at him, waiting for orders.

What were they doing? He eased up to get a visual. One beardless man held his flashlight under his arm while he lit a cigarette. The other two sported beards, like Brooke said.

Rex shifted his feet and a small twig snapped.

One of the men looked their direction. He stepped off the trail. "Did y'all hear that?"

"Hear what?"

The other two men followed and stopped just feet from where they hid. Flashlights swiped across the area. "Thought I heard something."

"You really think she got this far?" the other man asked, looking all around him.

"If the abandoned camp is any sign that she has help, then yeah. She could be right under our noses." The one smoking flicked his cigarette ashes.

Trent glanced down at Brooke. Her fear-filled eyes gripped his heart.

"Think she can ID us?" The one with a gruffy voice asked.

"She won't get away. Besides, nabbing her out here eliminates witnesses. No one will ever know what happened to her. When the police find Nick's body with those divorce papers on the floor, they'll assume she killed him and is on the run." The man's smooth tone lacked emotion. He took a long draw from his cigarette and blew out smoke. "Nick shouldn't have pressed his luck. If he couldn't pay, he shouldn't have placed the bet. We're getting that kid. I ain't losing five hundred K."

"You're splitting the money with us, right?" The other tall guy shifted his stance.

"Find the girl and we'll talk about it." The beardless guy turned. "Come on, let's double back and search that tent again. We need to know who we're dealing with." His flashlight flickered. He shook it. "My battery's going out. Guess we can get a little shut-eye and start searching again at dawn. I've read about this trail—it only leads one way, and that's over the mountain."

The man turned and stomped back through the tall grass to the trail. The others followed. "Let's go."

Fumes shot from Trent's ears. Brooke was right. They *were* after her baby. The beardless one seemed to know her husband. Did she know him? She'd said a voice sounded familiar.

She covered her mouth with one hand. Her tears dripped on the rock and showed up like crystals through his goggles. Her suffering stabbed at his heart, and he knew nothing about her. He imagined his sister when she gave birth to his niece. The thought of someone taking Mandy would have devastated her. He would give his life for his niece, like he would put his life on the line for Brooke and her unborn infant.

Trent dropped his shoulders. They had a reprieve for the moment. As soon as the men were farther down the trail and out of sight, he'd keep her moving.

Brooke held her abdomen, rocked back and forth. "This one's worse."

Full-blown labor would take over soon if she wasn't already there. How much longer could she walk? Regretfully, he had to come up with a delivery plan, just in case. Flashes of delivering that preemie at the wreck shot through his mind. CPR hadn't helped. The loss wrenched in his gut. He hadn't intended to be put in an emergency delivery situation again. If only he could walk away and leave her to fend for herself, but that would be cold and cruel. He and Rex were search and rescue, and she needed rescuing. Could he put his emotions aside and distance himself from her?

Chapter Three

Brooke lifted her head off the rock, swiped at her face to make sure no bugs crawled on her and cut her eyes up at Trent. "They're leaving?" she whispered. The cool night temperature on the mountain sent a chill over her and made her shiver. Mosquitos continued buzzing around her head. Could she die from too many mosquito bites?

He dug his backpack out from under the fallen tree and zipped it open. "I don't see their lights anymore so they should be a good distance away now." As she scratched her arm, he added, "Should've thought of mosquito spray earlier. It won't hurt the baby, so hold your arms out."

She didn't hesitate. If she had to count the bites on her bare arms, there must be a gazillion, and they itched.

He sprayed her arms and blocked her face with his hand when he sprayed her neck. He sprayed himself too, even on his clothes. Who would have thought she'd run into a cop in the forest? So far, he'd been respectful and helpful.

Rex ran over to the water and lapped up a drink.

Trent tugged at something in his bag. If only she had night goggles, too. "Here, you're shivering. Put this long-sleeved shirt on. Temperatures get down in the fifties after dark."

"Thanks." She slid her arms into the fabric. The instant warmth helped relax the outside chill, but nothing could alter the trepidation swirling through her veins.

He unzipped his lightweight jacket, slipped it off and handed it to her.

"No." She pushed it away. "You need it."

"You're wrapping up for two, remember? Take it. The shirt I have on is thicker than the one you're wearing."

His shirt and jacket hung almost to her knees in the back, but her belly took up some slack in the front. She rolled up the sleeves to find her hands. His jacket hadn't looked baggy on him back at the campfire. In fact, it fit snug against his broad shoulders and muscular biceps. With his height, he should've been a basketball player.

"We're safe for now?" She winced at the thought of the thugs returning.

"I think so, but keep your guard up. Talk low for safety's sake. Once they ransack my camp, they'll know I left in a hurry and will assume you're with me." He patted his bag. "All my identification is in this backpack."

"All my stuff is in my purse back in the cabin." She pushed to her feet. If Trent questioned her story, what if the other cops thought she killed Nick like those men said? Would they think she was dumb enough to flee and leave her driver's license behind? She fought the alarm invading her.

I'm so lost and scared right now.

Trent threw on his backpack and shortened Rex's leash. "Let's keep moving. Try to stay calm and focused. Come on, Rex."

His large hand found hers and tugged. Security was in his grip. Each step found uneven ground. Her thin sneakers didn't shield her feet from the rough, craggy surface. Would the hiking trail be smoother than trekking randomly through the forest?

If her parents knew what had happened, they'd be mortified. They understood her childhood experience with the bear and the nightmares that kept her from enjoying backyard campouts with her cousins. She would never have voluntarily stepped into the woods unless her life depended on it. But she had. All because of divorce papers.

Her thoughts soared. If Nick ran out of collateral for his gambling debt, had he bet against her bakery, too? Intense tightening hit her belly.

"Ugh." She pulled her hand from Trent's and hugged her abdomen.

Rex trotted up to her and nudged her hand.

"What's he doing?" She moved back.

"He senses your discomfort and wants to console you."

"Seriously? Dogs do that?" Brooke hesitated before dropping her hand and letting the dog sniff and lick it. She pulled back and wiped the wetness on her pants.

"Rex is a lot smarter than people know." His gaze

moved to her hands on her belly. "How long have these contractions been going on?"

She appreciated the concern in Trent's voice. "They're sporadic. Nothing regular yet." She straightened when the tightness released.

"As long as they stay irregular, we should be okay. Let me know when the pain and pressure increase."

"I refuse to have my baby out here." The idea of giving birth among the wildlife terrified her. Josiah's room was ready for his arrival. Soft blue blankets coordinated with white-and-blue onesies, a mobile over his bed with stars and clouds dancing around with the wind-up music. Not to mention the comfortable gliding rocker with navy cushions.

"And I don't want the responsibility of delivering him. Are you okay to keep going?"

Trent's comment pulled her thoughts from the baby's nursery. She was in the dark, and still in the woods. Thinking about peaceful things helped her cope.

"Okay as I can be, out here in this jungle."

Trent stumbled, jerking her forward. Rex gave a low bark. She grabbed his arm with her free hand and kept him from falling. "Are you okay?" she said. "Please don't get hurt. I'm enough of a problem right now."

"It's all good. Tree root snuck up on me. We're close to the trail."

"Thank the Lord." She brushed hair from her sweaty face. A ponytail holder would have been handy about now.

"Guess you're a church girl." Disappointment came in his tone. "Watch it right here—there are several rocks on the path."

"I grew up in church, so yeah. I take it you're not."

"I did once, but life happens, and things change." He was quiet for a moment. "To each his own."

"Something bad must have happened."

"No disrespect, but it's not up for discussion." He stopped. "There's a limb about head level. Don't let it hit you in the face."

She stretched her free hand out and took hold of the limb. The rough surface and prickly leaves slid through her hand. That would have hurt. "Any idea what time it is and how far we've gone?"

He dropped her hand. A small light displayed on his wrist. "A little after midnight. It's officially Saturday. We've only gone about a mile and a quarter. When daylight hits, maybe we can pick up the pace a little."

Who was he kidding? She was lucky to be standing right now.

"Your legs are longer than mine. If we go any faster, you'll have to drag me. I'd planned to go home tomorrow, well, this morning. Doesn't look like that's going to happen." She frowned. "Why do I keep hearing Nick's scream telling me to run, then gunshots?"

"You've been through a lot. Probably still in shock. Could be why you're having contractions, too."

"Are we going to walk all night? I mean, my legs feel like noodles. I don't know how much farther I can go after running through the woods for what seemed an eternity before I landed at your camp." She blew out a harried breath.

The moon shone through the trees, and she caught a glimpse of her surroundings. Rex led the way, still hooked to his leash. Trent's oversize backpack blocked her view of him. His tall stature gave her a sense of security. Not to mention his broad shoulders and the way his shirt tightened around his biceps. His messy dark hair and stubby beard caught her attention back at the campfire. She guessed his eyes were dark too, but she couldn't tell without proper lighting. Good-looking if she did say so.

Shadows from low-lying bushes were like animals ready to pounce. She looked up at the stars through the swaying tree limbs and leaves. Such a contrast of fear and peace.

He stopped and faced her. "Hadn't thought about that. I've been so focused on reaching the ranger's station that I hadn't considered the distance you'd already run. If you can make it a little longer, there's an abandoned cabin up ahead. We can hunker down for the night."

"I'll try. Think those men will come back and find us?"

"Not until dawn, but it's a chance we'll have to take." He took her hand again and pulled her forward. "Remember, I am a cop, I have a gun, and a protective K-9 partner. We'll be on the move by daybreak."

Her feet ached and her flat-soled shoes grew tighter. The swelling in her ankles had worsened. Why not, after all, she'd been on the run for three hours or more without a reasonable reprieve. *Focus on the cabin. It's just ahead. I can do this. I can. I'm so tired.*

How much farther? Her legs grew weaker. She trudged forward, keeping her thoughts on the cabin and resting. Lying on a wood floor never appealed to her before, but the thought of sleep, regardless of where, grew on her. Her back ached, and the baby kicked and punched.

Nick would never get to meet his son. Would Josiah's birth have changed his negative habits? Probably not. Apparently, he was in too deep. So many questions. How could he take part in a bet if he knew he couldn't pay up? Heat rose to her cheeks. How could anyone consider a baby as payment for anything? Ludicrous.

"Almost there," he said, tugging her to the right, through some tall grass. "This way, Rex." She stepped over several fallen tree limbs. Clouds blocked the once bright moon, forcing her to depend on Trent for directions. "We're at the front porch of the cabin. Can you see the step?"

"Barely." Anticipation of resting her legs pushed her up the wood step and through the door. The moldy, musty dampness curled her nose, but it was a castle compared to where she'd imagined sleeping before finding Trent. On the ground with wildlife all around.

"Shouldn't use a flashlight. I doubt anyone's brave enough to go hiking in the dark besides us and those men, but if they changed their minds and turned back around, they'll spot the light. Good thing is, my vision is clear with my goggles on. There's an old table and a couple of wooden chairs in here. It looks like a one-bedroom cabin. Let me scope it out before we settle in for the night."

His feet clomped, then tiptoed quietly across the wooden floor. Rex's nails tapped the floor as he followed Trent. She wrapped her arms around Josiah and lifted the pressure of his weight in her belly. Light scrapes and shuffling came from the dark room until Trent returned.

"Not much, but I found an old cot. I tried sitting, and it didn't rip, so you may not have to sleep on the floor after all." He placed the rickety bed along the inside living room wall. "Here, I have a few small bottles of water left. I don't need you to dehydrate, so drink this. You'll rest better."

"Thanks." She raked her hand across the rough fabric before she eased down on the cot. It creaked. Water never tasted so good. She set the bottle on the floor, lay back and willed herself to relax.

"What about you? Where will you sleep?"

"Rex and I will stand watch. He hears noises before I do." Trent patted the canine's side. "Don't you, boy? He's always alert and saves lives."

She squinted in the darkness and made out the shaded outline of Trent and his dog. The two were a pair. Must be nice to be loved that much.

Trent eyed Brooke lying on the cot. "I'm going to look around for a place to hide, should we need it. I'll be back in a sec."

He took careful steps to avoid his hiking boots clomping on the wood floor. The small linen closet might hold one person, but not all three of them. It wouldn't work. He returned to the living room. "Nothing in here—I'll look around outside the cabin." He hooked the leash back on Rex. "Come."

Rex sniffed the floor and wagged his tail.

"You're leaving me here, alone?" Fear emitted from her lips.

"Only for a minute. I'll be right outside. Not going far." He traipsed out the door and lengthened his dog's leash. Brooke had softened in her disapproval of Rex. A few more gentle nudges and his canine might win her trust.

Rex ran around in the tall grass, sniffing, wagging his tail and marking his territory. He curved back to Trent's side. From what Trent could tell with his goggles on, the cabin faced the trees, and the hiking trail was to the right. He turned and circled around to the other side of the cabin. An area with a lot of brush in the opposite direction of the trail had possibilities. He high-stepped the weeds a few paces and halted at a three-foot drop-off in the terrain. That would have to do.

Satisfied that he'd found a semi-safe hiding place, he went back inside and found Brooke sitting on the cot. "Anything wrong?"

"Just waiting for you to get back."

"I'm here now. You can relax." He unhooked Rex's leash. "Found a hiding place out back should we need it."

A wood table the size of a card table was close to the kitchen. It weighed more than Trent expected as he moved it and one chair close to the cracked, cob-webbed window and propped his feet up. Rex roamed around the cabin, checking things out, then stopped at the cot beside Brooke. "Over here, boy, leave her alone and let her rest."

Rex trotted to Trent's side and lay at his feet.

A direct view of the trail kept him abreast of anyone approaching from the south. He removed the goggles long enough to rub his eyes and put them back on. Daylight travel was the best time to hike, but it would put Brooke and him in the clear crosshairs of their pursuers. Not much he could do except keep his eyes open, watch Rex's responses and listen for approaching voices.

"Thank you for helping me. I hate that I've put you in danger. I'll never forgive myself if anything happens to you."

"Rex and I are a team and we volunteered, remember?"

She gave an uncertain nod and seemed lost in thought.

The three thugs flashed into his mind. "Did Nick always have a gambling problem?"

She shook her head. "He was a good man in the beginning. As time passed, he began hanging out at bars and coming home in the wee hours of the morning. Then, I began noticing a decline in our savings account and things around the house started disappearing. Like my diamond necklace and earrings he gave me as a wedding present. Just stuff."

"How'd you find out he was gambling?" Sounded like she'd had a rough time, and one of the roughest could be labor in the forest. His confidence had plummeted three weeks ago with that preemie. He'd avoid another delivery at all costs. If he paced it right, maybe they'd be able to make the trek to the ranger's station before the baby came.

"He brought plastic cups home from the casinos, so I knew what was happening, and his addiction only got worse. Then, I discovered I was pregnant and confronted him." She rubbed her hand over her belly. "I'm not due for two more weeks, but between the intermittent contractions and the stress, it could be anytime."

"How'd he react?" The more she shared the better he understood her situation.

"He didn't like it at first, but finally accepted the idea. Guess he thought I'd quit work and wouldn't get a paycheck, which would limit his extracurricular activities. He timed a lot of his outings around payday and blamed me for restricting his fun by trapping him with this baby. His accusations infuriated me. We agreed on having a baby for months. Once it happened, our lives changed, and we argued a lot. I dealt with his lies and cheating until I couldn't handle it anymore. So, I filed for divorce, but he kept procrastinating signing the papers."

"Addictions can change a person's personality. Seen it too many times. Drugs, gambling, the party scene. Sadly, the abuser gets pulled in and doesn't realize the escalation in his negative behavior."

She nodded. "Can we change the subject? To something more pleasant, like how in sync you and Rex seem. It's really something."

He rubbed his dog's head. "Yeah, Rex is my buddy. I told you before that he senses danger, fear and pregnancy, too."

"He knows I'm pregnant. How?" Her curiosity intrigued him. "You said he sensed my discomfort, earlier."

"For canines, pregnancy changes the scent of a woman. That's why he keeps trying to sniff your legs and abdomen. He knows you're fragile and that you're afraid of him."

"Interesting. I had no clue."

"Most animals, domestic or wild, can sense fear or weakness, rather, vulnerability. That's why it's important to stand tall and don't cower when confronted. Otherwise, you could bring trouble on yourself."

She looked away for a moment. "Can I ask you a personal question?

"Sure."

"Anyone special in your life? Married? Girlfriend? Kids?" Her voice barely above a whisper.

He stared out the window at the swaying trees. A few leaves blew across the overgrown ground in front of the cabin. Did he want to discuss his personal life and past relationship? Nope.

"Almost married once," he said despite himself. "A large corporation offered her a lucrative job in Texas. She wanted me to come with her. Our relationship might have worked out, but I wouldn't let go of my position as a K-9 handler in Chattanooga. We dissolved our relationship a couple of years ago and said our goodbyes. That was that." He raked fingers through his hair. The breakup still stung. "You best get some rest while you can."

"Sorry it didn't work out. That's a hard decision to make when you care about someone." She lay back and let out a deep sigh. "I can't thank you enough for…" Her voice trailed off, and she fell silent.

His muscles twitched. He had avoided getting involved with another woman, even though he longed to settle down and have a family. Sure, they'd discussed a long-distance relationship, but it wouldn't work. She'd chosen her career over him and he'd chosen his life in

Chattanooga over moving for her. Kind of like Brooke's husband chose gambling over his family. Emptiness plagued him. Maybe one day.

He glanced at Brooke's baby bump, then back out the window at the dark forest. If she knew his last delivery hadn't gone as planned, she'd be more distressed. The first baby he delivered while on the job was healthy and had the lungs of an opera singer. Maybe not that much. He'd soared with joy, but losing the preemie had him hesitant and leery of ever doing it again. Brooke's eyes had exhumed uncertainty, and yet, confidence in him. He *knew* how to deliver her baby, if need be, but he'd avoid it if possible. Just the thought of it sent a surge of nausea through him and twisted every muscle in his body.

Brooke curled up on the cot and held her abdomen, apparently still having contractions. He eased over and checked on her. Did he have the nerve to touch her belly and check the tightness? Better not. Might frighten her and make her scream. He let out an exhausted sigh and returned to his chair. He stared through the trees until he spotted some stars. Was God out there somewhere waiting for him to mess up again?

Since she apparently trusts, You, God, don't let her go into labor on my watch. You know how that would turn out. And you might keep her out of sight of these killers if you want her safe.

He yawned. Wasn't the way he wanted to die.

Watching the forest all night gave him a lot of time to think. Too much. He had insisted on being alone on this trip, even though his parents warned him of the dangers. He'd given them all the details of his trail, campsite and when he'd planned to return. This trip was the getaway he needed to get his head straight about his job and refocus. So much for that.

He hadn't gotten his EMT license to deliver babies. He only wanted to assist in minor medical situations when needed. Guilt over losing the infant ate at him. No one could ever know the pain and disappointments he and his coworkers took home when things went wrong on the job. Doubt arose for him when the situation required confidence and quick thinking. Instead, the flashbacks slowed his responses. His sergeant had noticed his hesitance and offered him time off to deal with it. How could he ever get past the disappointment that loomed over him?

If he transferred to the training center and assisted with handlers and canines, that would remove him from the streets. He scratched his head. Maybe not. They could still call him out on urgent missions. Besides, he loved being out in the field and spending time in the wilderness. He couldn't and wouldn't do anything to risk losing Rex.

The dog jumped to his feet and growled.

"Quiet." Trent squinted behind his goggles. Movement outside pushed him to his feet and into the dark shadows of the cabin. The hair on his arms lifted with a domino effect. Rex watched him, waiting for a command. His heart exploded in his chest as he peered around the edge of the window, fully expecting to find the three men standing there. A large, majestic specimen of an elk stood close to the steps with his head held high. He moved forward and munched on grass as he made his way across the trail and out of sight. Trent's shoulders relaxed, and he holstered his weapon.

Rex ran to the door and whined.

"Come here." Trent patted the side of his leg. He bent and patted the dog's side. "Just an elk. Do you need to go outside?"

Rex wagged his tail and danced in place while Trent put the leash on him and extended the length. He stepped out on the porch, leaving the cabin door open in the cool of the wee hours, and breathed in the fresh air. Rex explored the area and marked his territory in several places.

Trent's thoughts drifted to the young pregnant widow sleeping inside. She mentioned witnessing a bear attack years ago. No wonder she was so rigid with nature. He'd ask for more details when timing was right.

He tugged at the leash, and Rex ran back up the steps and into the cabin. He closed the door, unleashed his canine, then eased down on the hard chair. Rex plopped down in the middle of the room. Dawn would break soon. Prime time for wildlife to stir and look for food, and that included bears. His biggest concern.

Brooke suddenly gasped and sat up, with her eyes still closed.

Rex jumped to his feet with a growl.

"Sit." Trent whispered. "Keep quiet."

"Run," she said, her eyes still closed. "Don't think about bears, just run. They killed Nick." Her hands stretched out in front of her, and she mimicked pushing objects from her face. "Have to protect my baby." Her feet moved like she was running. Then they stopped. She lay back down. "Trent will protect me."

She mumbled other undecipherable words. He bit his lip. Somehow, he'd made his way into her dreams. Shock and fear of Nick's murder and the unknown probably played into her nightmare. Could he save her? Between Rex and him, they'd do the best they could to keep her and Josiah safe. He blew out an exhausted breath and checked his watch. Almost four in the morning.

He removed the night goggles and laid them on the table, rubbed his eyes so long he almost fell asleep. All had been quiet, and he was thankful. Brooke had about three hours of sleep. Restless, but she'd slept. How long could *he* go without some shut-eye? Maybe those two energy drinks would keep him awake.

His eyes rolled. He stretched his arms up in the air, then down, and popped his neck, slid down in the hard chair and laid his head on the wood back, still watching out the window. The trees tossed. A storm must be approaching. That's all they needed to hinder their hike. Wet trails meant more problems.

The silence gave him too much time to think. Clouds covered the moon briefly and moved on. Turmoil over getting Brooke to safety kept him awake. He couldn't sleep if he had the opportunity, besides, he couldn't risk another nightmare with her around.

Rex nudged Trent's arm and growled.

Voices. Had he heard voices? Trent stood and shoved his goggles into the backpack. Sure enough. In the distance, the three men traipsed up the trail. His pulse raced.

Any noise at this point could alert them to movement inside the cabin. "Come." He ordered Rex. The hollow echo of footsteps in a deserted cabin was like talking through a megaphone. He tiptoed to Brooke's side and touched her shoulder.

"Brooke, wake up." Her eyes popped open. He put a finger to his lips. "Shhh, they're back and headed this way. Implement Plan B."

She gasped and stared at him, wide-eyed. "What's Plan B?" She whispered.

"Out the back door and hide. Be quiet." He rushed to the window. Goose bumps crawled up his spine. He could throw a rock and hit them. They were close. Too close.

He hooked the leash on Rex's collar. "Quiet. I'll let you know if I need your assistance." He tossed his pack over his shoulder and onto his back.

Brooke slid to her feet, holding her belly. His heart went out to her. Just when she should be eagerly anticipating the arrival of her newborn, she was running for her life. She moved without a sound to the back door and opened it.

His eyes shifted to the cot. If they came inside and touched the fabric, they'd feel the warmth of where she slept. He lifted the cot and turned it bottom side up. Maybe the floor would cool it down so they wouldn't notice. Another glance outside revealed they'd stopped on the trail and pointed toward the cabin. Just as he expected, they'd be on the porch step at any moment.

The taller guy carried something on his back that he hadn't had earlier. Looked like a tent. Really? Had they taken his tent? He fumed at their audacity and followed Brooke out the back door. He closed it quietly, then took Brooke's hand and rushed her through the tall grass. He hopped down the small dip and helped her down. Rex jumped into the hole with them and stood beside Trent with his head tall and ears up.

He motioned for Rex to lie down, then helped Brooke sit on the ground and he joined her. A frown moved across her face as she grabbed her abdomen. Now wasn't a good time for contractions. He placed his hand on her arm. *Don't let her scream. Make these pains stop.* He'd just prayed again. What kind of influence was she having on him? A good one he guessed.

He looked at Brooke and studied her features for the first time in the daylight. The swelling had subsided from around her eyes, and she had a clear complexion. Her eyes were the color of a cloudless sky. Bluer than blue and her long brown hair framed her face, only adding to her natural beauty. Was he admiring her? Yes. He looked away.

The sound of wood banging against wood redirected his attention. Their pursuers had thrust the front door of the cabin open. Tromping footsteps roamed the cabin. The back door opened, and one man stepped outside.

"No signs of them. Must have bypassed the cabin," one said.

"Found a water bottle. Somebody's been here." The gruffy voice stung his ears.

Trent scolded himself. He'd forgotten about the water bottle he'd given Brooke. Wasn't like him to allow distractions. Could be anyone's bottle since she didn't have lipstick on. He breathed a sigh of relief, grabbed his cell and tried to take a picture of the guy, but the grass and weeds were too thick. He couldn't risk raising his cell higher.

The man with a smooth-sounding voice stepped out the back door. "Could be anybody's empty bottle. We might've caught up with them by now if we hadn't gone back to that campsite. No more stopping. This trail only leads one way, so we're on the right track. If we get rid of whoever's helping her, it'll slow her down even more."

The door slammed and their voices faded.

"Don't move." Trent whispered in her ear. "I'm going to see where they went." He took off his backpack and laid it aside.

Rex hopped to his feet with his head held high. He sniffed the air.

"Stay. Quiet."

Brooke pressed her lips together, looked at Rex and back at him. A black ant crawled up her arm. She slapped it off and shivered. A few days out in the elements and she'd either loathe nature with a viable reason or learn the ropes of hiking and being resourceful and finding the beauty in it.

Trent crawled through the tall grass and pulled the blades apart just enough to get a visual. The three killers reached the trail and picked up their pace, climbing the mountain Brooke and he had yet to climb. He clenched his jaw and returned to where she hid.

"Okay, you can come out now," he said in a low voice. "They're gone."

She didn't move.

"Brooke?"

She slapped at her clothes, rolled onto her knees and tried pushing herself up. Trent caught her arm and helped. "Thought there was a spider on my shirt, and I was afraid to move." She stood, brushed dirt from her clothes, placed her hands at her sides and stretched her back. My legs feel a little stronger today. I'm sore, but I think I'm okay."

"Good. That's really good. Because the next leg of our journey is uphill and that's the direction Zeke and the other two guys went." He pointed her toward the cabin. "Let's go back inside for a few minutes."

"Which means we will be behind them." Her big blue eyes searched him.

"Yes, and it could be to our advantage." Trent grabbed his backpack and followed her inside. They had a long journey ahead. He'd do what he could to get her back to her family.

Chapter Four

Brooke kept watch out the back window of the cabin while Trent emptied the contents of his backpack on the small table. A spiderweb mixed with dust found a home across the faucet. She backed away.

"Will they hear us coming up behind them? I'm still trying to place the man with the familiar voice." She took in a deep breath. Was this nightmare really happening? About this time yesterday morning she was enjoying a hot cinnamon roll and a caramel latte with an employee in the cool, clean atmosphere of her bakery. They'd know something was wrong when she didn't show up for her Danish, something she'd craved all through her pregnancy.

Josiah punched her belly. She rubbed circles over her abdomen and patted gently. "Hold on, little guy. We've got to get over this mountain. Just a little longer."

"What's a little longer?" Trent flipped the backpack around.

"Oh, just talking to Josiah." Did he think she was strange talking to her unborn baby? "Did you know an unborn baby can hear what's being said on the outside? They sense what's happening and can feel what I feel? Guess that's why people read books to their babies before they're born. Sounds silly, doesn't it?"

"So, I've heard. That's why I always greeted my niece while Dana was pregnant. Probably why she loves me best." He chuckled and glanced her direction. "As long as those guys don't decide to backtrack again, we should be okay. There's no way to know. Gotta keep moving, though. Every step forward is a step closer to getting you help."

She joined him at the table. The morning light had her noting his height and how well-built he was. His green eyes stood out against tanned skin and dark brown hair. She redirected her eyes and observed his supplies.

"We have a can of bug spray, one metal coffee cup, a two-cup coffee pot, folding spoon and fork. A small propane cooker. A lightweight tarp, first aid kit, six bottles of water, two energy drinks, beef jerky, peanut butter and crackers, trail mix, energy bars and two apples."

"Sounds like you packed plenty." Not the kind of meals she would have packed for a trip, but at least they wouldn't starve.

Rex appeared more accepting of her today. Had she earned his trust? Every time she looked at him, he turned his head and looked back at her, with his ears up as though he had eyes on the back of his head. He'd licked her hand last night and hadn't growled at her lately. Trent said he was super smart. She admired his black-and-tan coat.

Trent unzipped another section of his bag and pulled

out six small packets of dog energy bites, water bowl, eight meal replacement bars and half a package of dog treats. Looked like he'd packed more for his dog than he had for himself. He tossed Rex a dog meal replacement bar and stuffed some treats into his pocket.

She pulled off the jacket he'd loaned her. "Here, I don't need this today. I'll hang on to your shirt if that's okay."

"Sure. Just let me know if you get too cool."

He stuffed the jacket into the pack and pulled out a rolled-up plastic bag. "This is my comfort package from my four-year-old niece, with her mom's help, no doubt. Otherwise, I wouldn't be toting a small doll with a miniature bottle held on with this pink stretchy thing twisted on its wrist and wrapped in a thin blue blanket in my bag. If any of my coworkers saw it, I'd be the joke of the K-9 unit." He held up a scribbled note written with crayon in his sister's handwriting and read it out loud. "It says 'So you won't be lonely. Love Mandy.' My sister, Dana, added, 'She insisted. Be safe.'" He grinned.

"That's so sweet." Brooke smoothed her hand over the baby blanket. Her heart warmed at the love this child showed for her uncle and his understanding response.

"Funny how God used a child to meet a possible need."

He cleared his throat and held the doll out toward her. "You think God did this?"

"Who else do you think prompted your niece to hide her baby in your bag, on this trip?" She held her hand out. "Mind if I use the scrunchie? You know. It's that pink stretchy thing."

"Is that what you call this colored rubber band?" He handed it to her.

She finger-combed her matted hair as best she could and pulled it up into a ponytail. The scrunchie was almost too small, but she managed. Her stomach soured at the thought of not being able to shower and wash her hair. No hand sanitizer either. Ugh.

"Dana instigates the whole thing." He stuffed the doll, bottle and blanket inside the sack and shoved it back into his bag. "They're always doing goofy stuff like that. Last time, she sent a stuffed animal about the size of my hand."

"She's teaching her to care for others. I think it's wonderful. Sounds like Mandy and your sister love you very much." Brooke rubbed her abdomen again. "Maybe Josiah will be caring and giving, like them."

"Sun's just over the horizon." He handed her a packet of peanut butter sandwich crackers and a bottled water and began repacking his backpack. "Peanut butter is full of protein. Eat up, then we'll go. If we find some berries along the way, I'll grab a few."

"I don't want to take your food. Maybe we should save it for later." Who was she fooling? She had to have food and water, especially in her condition. Her stomach rumbled. Wasn't the meal she preferred, but it would have to do. A hot cup of coffee would be heaven about now.

"Like it or not, we're a team in survival mode, and we have to share everything until we get out of here. Had I known I'd be feeding two instead of one, I wouldn't have eaten all the prepackaged tuna and saltines."

"Are you eating?" A sense of intrusion swept over

her. She'd destroyed his restful camping trip. Could she ever make it up to him? She ripped the peanut butter cracker package open and took a bite. The salty flavor awakened her taste buds.

When was the last time she had eaten a complete meal? Yesterday, Friday, at lunch with her mom. Chicken salad sandwiches on a croissant. Her mouth watered. Seemed longer than that. If only she could talk to her mom right now. Her parents would bombard the mountains with an army of helicopters and men with assault rifles if they knew her predicament. Her mom's protective nature wouldn't hold back. Like how Brooke felt about Josiah. She'd protect her baby, regardless of her fears.

"I feel bad pulling you into this mess. I don't know how to thank you." She chewed on her lip and focused on keeping her emotions in check. Tears wouldn't help.

"Rex and I chose to help you." He didn't look up. "One small tarp, an extra pair of shoes, a lighter, another shirt and a pair of jeans." He patted his pocket, then his two holsters. "Knife and compass, here. Ruger .45 caliber here and Glock 19 here."

"Why two guns?"

"Self-defense. One is for large game and the other for humans." He lifted his eyebrows. "I don't intend to use either unless absolutely necessary."

Her knees weakened at the thought. One killing was enough.

"You're carrying all those supplies in that one bag? Isn't it heavy?"

"If you position it right, it's not any heavier to me

than it is for you carrying the full weight of your baby, only this pack is on my back, which makes it easier."

He rubbed Rex's head, tossed his ears around and looked him in the face. "Rex and I go everywhere together." He patted his furry sides and ruffled his fur.

Trent showed all the signs of being trustworthy, but so had Nick when they married. She studied the weapons and observed his mannerisms. He had all the qualifications of a protector. Why was he out here alone? He was likable enough, but at this point in her life, she couldn't trust her own instincts.

Trent unwrapped his energy bar and took a bite. He folded the paper over the top and stuck the rest in his shirt pocket. He assured her he'd hiked this trail before and said he knew the way out.

She didn't pretend to know about survival in the woods or how to deal with the wildlife. Besides her faith, her safety rested on his shoulders. A cop, but still a stranger. When she got home, if Nick hadn't already emptied their savings, she'd withdraw a nice lump sum and pay Trent for his selfless act of mercy and for losing his tent.

Her crackers disappeared too quickly. She took a few gulps of water and handed him the bottle. "Would you hold this for me?"

"Sure." He slid the bottle in a holder that looped around his waist, picked up Rex's empty bowl and stuck it in a side pocket of his backpack. "Let's go."

Rex trotted to the door and barked, wagging his tail. Trent hooked the leash to his collar and opened the door. Brooke stalled at the thought of leaving the cabin.

"What is it?" He eyed her.

"The cabin feels safe. Couldn't we wait here for help to arrive?"

He stepped into her personal space, took her hand and smoothed his thumb over her fingers. His green eyes pierced hers, and she gulped. "We could stay here, but no one knows where we are. We could be here for days with nobody but the killers passing on the trail. Every step up the mountain is a step closer to getting help." His words were soft, but to the point.

His warm hand gently touching hers sent a surge through her. She pulled her hand away and shifted her eyes. He was right and she couldn't argue the fact. She didn't want to leave the security and shelter of the cabin, but she had no choice. Her life and safety depended on the wisdom of this handsome K-9 handler and his dog.

Brooke eased out the front door. A tightness formed in her chest. She stepped as high as her legs allowed and walked through the tall grass. Trent paused and picked up two long limbs. He ripped leaves and smaller branches from the limbs and handed her one.

"Use this like a walking stick to help maintain your balance. People do it all the time." He turned and started up the path, with Rex leading the way.

"I need all the help I can get." She wrapped her hand around the smooth branch, poked it at the ground a few times and pressed forward, making sure each step landed flat on the ground. She'd do anything to keep from tripping over rocks and tree roots jutting above the soil. Falling wouldn't end well for her and could hurt Josiah.

They'd only walked a short distance when they

reached the base of an incline along the path. A weathered small maroon sign with barely legible white lettering marked the name of the trail, Redbud Trail. Excitement stirred, and her pulse increased. The first sign of civilization she'd seen since daylight. She swatted at insects flying too close to her head.

"Does this sign mean we're getting closer to help?" *Say yes.*

His glance back at her, and the solemn look on his face answered her question without a response. "Don't go getting your hopes up. It means we're leaving Chilhowee Mountain and beginning our first long, uphill trek into the Smoky Mountains. We still have five and a half miles to go, and this climb alone will take us a good four to six hours, depending on how well you hold up."

"Six hours?" The words choked in her throat. She jabbed her stick into the ground and took another step. "Couldn't you soften the truth a little? Just tell me a little farther or around the curve or something." She blew a stray strand of hair from her face.

"I'll keep that in mind next time you ask. Figured you wanted the truth, regardless."

"I do. Maybe not so abrupt. I'm totally out of my comfort zone." Living with Nick's lies had her conditioned to read between the lines. Her ability to decipher the truth increased through the years. Of course, she wanted the truth. Didn't she? Maybe not so much out here in the wild. What she didn't know couldn't frighten her any more than she was already.

A bird sang its tune somewhere in the trees. Another bird from the opposite direction sang as though responding to the first. Their melody offered little peace. She breathed in the fresh scent of honeysuckle and scanned the path for signs of animal tracks.

"Out of all your camping trips, have you had encounters with bears?"

"I've seen several black bears every time I hike up here, but I've never had a problem with them. You mind your business, most of the time they mind theirs, unless you get too close to a cub. That's where people get into trouble."

"No worries there. I'll stay as far away as possible." She cringed. The mere thought of wild animals close by caused nightmares and pushed her close to hyperventilation.

A cool breeze blew across her face, drying rolling perspiration. Tall trees swayed with the wind like a hula dance in slow motion, tossing their limbs. Various shades of green painted her surroundings. Ferns, vines and occasional wildflowers decorated the scenic view like a well-planned landscape job. If she weren't running for her life, she might consider admiring it more.

Her legs burned with each step, and her pace slowed. "You must have trained for hiking marathons or something. You make it look so easy with your even pace and steady climbing." She paused, wiped her forehead and caught her breath. The pressure of Josiah made her back ache.

Rex spun. His ears fell back, and he bared his teeth in a growl. She froze. Was he growling at her? What had she done? He rushed down the trail toward her. She braced herself for the attack. He ran past her as far as his leash allowed, jumping and barking ferociously.

"Rex. Quiet. Come here," Trent ordered in a stern

tone. "Brooke, take slow steps toward me." His sudden switch to a calm, steady voice told her not to run or make any sudden moves.

A snort and heavy breathing came from a thicket.

Chills rushed down her spine. Her feet wouldn't move, and her heart thrashed in her ears. She turned slowly and glanced behind her. A gasp escaped. A black bear walked leisurely up the trail behind them. Trent stepped beside her, holding his pistol. He lifted his arms and thrust them toward the bear. "Out of here, bear. Go. Get out."

A gravelly growl emitted from Rex.

The bear stopped, stood on his hind legs, sniffed and dropped back to his all fours. He turned and disappeared into the woods.

Her body trembled. A bear sneaking up behind her was the very thing she'd feared since she was eight years old. How much closer would the bear have gotten if Rex hadn't looked back. She imagined its massive claws coming down on her.

Her shaky hand grabbed Trent's muscular arm. "You saved me again. Thank you." She released her grip. "How did you know he wouldn't attack?"

"First, Rex heard the bear before either of us. He alerted me danger was approaching. If it weren't for him, we wouldn't be standing here right now. The advice posted at the ranger's station about what to do when coming face to face with a black bear proved true. Raise your hands and make noise." He patted Rex's head. "Thanks for the warning."

"But what you did took bravery. I can't believe you told the bear to go away, and he did."

"Thanks, but Rex gets the credit for his keen hearing and awareness of our surroundings. I just did what you're supposed to do when a bear approaches. Too bad they don't have easy steps for delivering babies in the woods." Anything could go wrong with no paramedics to assist. He turned and started up the trail. "Stay alert. Early mornings bring out the wildlife. They're scrounging for food. What's the deal with bears, anyway? You keep bringing them up."

She cleared her throat. "When I was eight years old, I was on a camping trip with my cousin. I spotted a bear cub and walked closer to get a good picture. The mom came barreling out of the thicket toward me. A bystander pushed me out of the way and the bear attacked him. It was my fault. I'd been told to stay away, but I didn't listen. The man survived, but the incident was bad enough that it instilled a lifelong fear in me. I never wanted to see the woods again."

"An incident like that could mar your opinion of nature and cause nightmares, especially at a young age."

"Yep. Nightmares have followed me into adulthood. That's why I stay in the city and do all my sightseeing downtown. Furry animals of any size or shape creep me out, including Rex. Albeit, he hasn't done anything to make me not like him. And I am thankful his hearing is better than mine."

Trent gripped her hand and gently helped her with the climb. His long fingers curled around her palm offered a small sense of his strength and security. She admitted having Rex along added an extra measure of precaution, and maybe, assurance. Was he trained to sense other animals and keep them alerted, or was it a natural reaction?

"Exactly what wildlife are you talking about?" She'd heard horror stories of people being attacked by animals or a pack of coyotes. The hair on her arms prickled at the thought. "I prefer visiting the zoo, where they're all in cages or behind thick glass. That's the only wildlife I care to see."

"There are no cages out here. There are bears, bob-cats, white-tailed deer, elk, wild hogs, groundhogs, chipmunks, squirrels and snakes, but I don't think you want to know about those." He chuckled.

"Not funny." She huffed and tried steadying her breathing. Her body rebelled at the uphill climb.

At least he didn't act annoyed. He seemed rather amused by her. She relaxed a little. The soreness in her thighs argued with each step. Between her walking stick and his tight grip pulling her uphill, they'd progressed a suitable distance, or so she thought.

"Oh." She came to an abrupt halt and jerked her hand from his. "No." She held her belly, took in a slow breath, and released it. *Don't go into labor.*

He stepped down the trail beside her and placed his hand on her back for a moment, then dropped it. "Just breathe.

His gentle touch made her fully aware of his close-ness. Her face warmed a bit, and it wasn't the August heat. The pain eased. She straightened and took in a few breaths, reached out and took his hand again. "At least we've made it this far without a pain. Maybe they'll be slower today."

"That's what we want. I'm not delivering a baby out

here. When they come at regular intervals and grow closer, we'll know it's the real thing."

"Agreed. Like I said earlier, I'm not having any part of birthing my baby in the wild." She pursed her lips, pushed herself up the rising trail behind him. The relentless pain in her low back refused to let up. What did he mean he wouldn't deliver her baby? Wasn't he trained for emergency situations, including deliveries? She lowered her eyebrows and pondered his comment.

Trent checked his watch. Nearing ten o'clock. He'd best keep track of her contractions. Dread crept up his spine at the likelihood of delivering her baby without the proper supplies. He'd done it before but had determined never again. Conditions were against him and his confidence had taken a hit. He shoved the thought to the back of his mind as best he could, but every glance in her direction reminded him of the impending task.

He forced himself to focus on getting her up the first incline. One step at a time, one hill at a time. They would get there. Maybe.

He looked back. Her almond-shaped eyes were still the bluest he'd ever seen, and her long brown hair bounced in the ponytail, bound by Mandy's pink scrunchie. The radiance in her face, which also emanated pain and sadness, confirmed reports that pregnant women had a glow about them.

"Are you making it okay?" Dumb question. Her slow pace and constant holding her abdomen told him she was doing the best she could.

"What do you think?" Her curt, breathless reply confirmed his assessment of her.

He ached for her desperate situation. She didn't deserve the trauma she'd endured. Hiking a moderately strenuous trail at this stage of her pregnancy didn't help. In fact, best he remembered, walking helped bring labor on quicker, which they couldn't avoid. Despite her apparent fears of the outdoors, she had a calmness about her that relaxed him. Well, except for the contractions and her dislike of Rex.

She couldn't know his biggest disaster and how guilt and sorrow over the preemie's death held him hostage. Like it took a plug out of his heart. He loved children and elation shot through him when he delivered a healthy baby, but having an infant die in his arms pushed past his macho attitude, tore at his emotions and undermined his self-confidence in the job he loved. He didn't want Brooke freaking out should an emergency arise. He'd stored his failures and downfalls in his mental record book, and he didn't need anyone's pity.

"My bad. You're having a difficult time." He pressed forward. "You know, I've always liked my job. It's rewarding when Rex and I find lost children and track down Alzheimer's patients who have wandered away from home, but ushering a pregnant lady seven miles over a mountain on the run from killers is a first. Saving lives and returning loved ones safely home brings a sense of accomplishment. Like we've just made the world a better place." He couldn't fail. Not this time. He told her he'd get her over the mountain to safety, and he always tried to keep his word.

"I think what you do is admirable. Must be a rewarding feeling to see the relief and joy in those families faces. Returning home to a loving home is priceless."

He eased around a pile of loose rocks. "Watch your step." His thoughts soared. At least Brooke had a baby to love. He only had his parents, siblings and a beautiful niece. His tough-guy heart melted around kids and he longed to settle down and have his own someday.

"Talk to me," she said, pulling him from his thoughts. "I need to focus on something besides animals creeping up behind me." She breathed heavily with each step. "Tell me about Rex."

"Rex is a smart canine. He's assisted me in the rescue of a child who disappeared from the park at one of the local preschools. Rex sniffed the child's sweater and tracked her trail. We came to a small shallow stream and thought we'd lost her scent. Rex stepped in the water and kept walking, sniffing both sides of the water until he picked the scent up again. His ears perked up and he took off running, then stopped and sat with his head straight. The child had crawled into a box beside a dumpster. She was dirty, but safe and unharmed. He's an excellent search and rescue canine."

"That's amazing. Are all police dogs trained to do that or is it a natural instinct?"

"They all go through training for their specific task. Some catch on quick while others take a little more work. Rex is intelligent. He follows my lead and responds according to my reactions and behavior toward people. When he accepts others as part of his pack, he will protect them, too."

"Are you still trying to figure me out? He seems to accept me, but you know him better than I."

"If I didn't believe your story, I wouldn't have gotten involved and Rex wouldn't have warmed up to you.

We just met last night. Friendships and trust develop over time."

"Friendships. I agree. Complete trust? Never."

Change the subject. Trent searched his thoughts.

"Rex loves the forest. If you notice, his nose goes from the air to the ground, sniffing in all the scents. Trees, dirt, plants, flowers and, of course, wildlife. He traipses back and forth across the trail, checking things out and looking back at me for approval. Best decision I ever made was teaming up with him."

Rex glanced back, but continued up the path. His mouth open, tongue hanging out as he panted and ears up. Man's best friend was correct.

"In fact, our police K-9 unit earned the Overall Top Dog award last year." The wind picked up. He looked at the sky. "Clouds are rolling in. Looks like a storm's brewing."

"I don't need more trouble. I have enough of my own."

Rex tugged on the leash, barked and growled.

"Here." Trent pointed to the ground directly in front of him. Rex obeyed. He sat and looked up, waiting for instructions. A rattling noise interrupted the silence of the woods. Trent straightened and held his arm out toward her.

"What is it? What did he see?" Brooke stepped closer. Her hand rested on his forearm.

"Rattlesnake up ahead. If I give the order, Rex and the rattlesnake would be at war. No way am I putting him in striking distance of this snake. Move slow. We won't bother him if he doesn't bother us."

"Are you serious?" She whispered. "My heart is

pounding out of my chest and the hair on my arms is standing straight up. What are you going to do? Can you shoot it?"

"A gunshot would alert anyone within hearing range to where we are. If those men weren't an issue, then the shot would prove beneficial." He pulled his pistol. "Ease around the side of the trail with me." Her grip tightened. He reeled Rex closer to his leg and pushed Brooke behind him, shielding her and his dog from a strike. They stepped off the opposite side of the trail. "Sidestep slowly with me while I keep my eyes on the snake."

Rex growled.

She dropped her hold on his arm and squeezed his shoulder like her life depended on it, and it did. Rattlers were deadly. She stayed in sync with his every move like they were slow dancing. Rex begged to sink his teeth into the serpent.

"Good. Easy now. A little more." Maybe his instructions and soft tone would prevent her from screaming or making any sudden moves.

The snake rattled, letting Trent know it was aware of their presence. He winced when her fingernails dug into his shoulder. His heart pounded like a war dance in his ears. He pushed her back another couple of steps and sidestepped up the trail, leaving the snake behind. When they were a safe distance away, he took her hand off his shoulder. "We're good now."

"Are you sure it's gone? Will it follow us? Are there more? Of course, there are more, we're in the mountains. Ugh, that freaks me out. This is another reason I couldn't live in the mountains or go camping, but I'm surprised it didn't chase after us."

"You have to respect its personal space. I love the mountains. Camping helps me clear my mind. Whatever you do, don't panic. Staying calm in any situation can help save your life." He slid his gun back into the holster, lengthened the leash for Rex and stretched his arm out toward Brooke. He took her hand. "Let's keep moving. We need to pick up the pace."

Her walking stick hit his foot a few times as she stayed on his heels for the next few steps. How could he distract her? He could tell her a little bit about himself, nothing too personal.

"My parents live in Chattanooga," he said. "I have a brother and a sister and a niece, as you know. My brother married his high school sweetheart, but they don't have any children. My dad is an airplane mechanic, and my mom left her job as an administrative assistant for a corporation to stay home and babysit my niece while Dana works. She's a nurse-practitioner at a doctor's office." He stopped. "Watch this uneven area. There're a lot of holes."

She shoved her stick into the ground and trudged forward. "You and your sister are in the essential employees category. There's nothing essential about owning a bakery other than offering a sugar rush to my patrons. You do important work serving others. That's so cool. Being a K-9 cop is an admirable job. You should be proud of your accomplishments. I bet it gets tough sometimes."

She didn't know the half of it. He loved his work, but it had more dangers and stresses she'd never relate to.

His shoulders tensed with every contraction she had. Another part of his job he hadn't asked for on his camping trip. Mixed emotions about their situation had him huffing and clenching his teeth.

"Has its downside," he said.

"Your parents sound wonderful. They must be extremely proud of you."

He shot her a glance as they walked. Her eyes were on the path, watching her feet. Warmth rose to his cheeks. And it wasn't because of the humidity. He refused to look back again, or she might see him blushing. His parents and sister bragged on him occasionally, but it wasn't the same as hearing accolades from someone he was just getting to know, someone he was responsible for.

"I guess. What about you? Where's your family?"

"Ouch." She held his arm and lifted one foot. "Almost twisted my ankle. That smarts."

"You okay?" If only he could carry her. She'd done well to get this far. They'd go as far as he could press her. She eased her foot to the ground and moved her leg around.

"I think so. Maybe I can walk it out." She dropped her hand and limped a short distance. "My parents and two sisters, Beth and Hannah, live a couple of miles from me. My dad works with an architectural firm, and my mom helps me at the bakery sometimes. She was a stay-at-home mom. We loved her being there when we got home from school. She never expressed an interest in working an outside job." She stopped, bent over slightly and groaned. "Hang on."

Trent checked his watch and searched the cloudy sky

again. It had been about thirty minutes since her last contraction. "We should take a break."

"I'd like that." She blew out a few slow breaths before straightening. "I barely feel my legs and the swelling in my feet is getting worse."

Not a good sign this close to delivery. Severe swelling could cause complications. "There's a small clearing up ahead. We can stop and rest a minute."

"So, you said you weren't delivering my baby if I go into labor before we get to the ranger's station. Why?"

Rex's ears straightened and fell back. He whined.

Trent stiffened and not just because of her question. "Voices," he whispered. His pulse picked up speed. Their pursuers had returned. "It's them. They're coming back down the trail toward us." He stepped off the path, still holding her hand. "Come on."

Against his better judgment, he led her through the tall grass and around some large boulders. Ideal hiding places for snakes. He studied the ground, noting bear scat in a couple of places. "Not here." No need to tell her why.

Another boulder approximately sixteen feet tall protruded from the mountainside. Rex trotted ahead, checking out the area. Trent stepped around the stone and halted at the edge of a cliff. Just enough room to sit on the ground, out of sight. He placed his backpack in the dirt and had Brooke sit on it, then pointed. "Rex, sit."

Rex sat at Brooke's side. She lifted her arm like she didn't know what to do with it with Rex so close. He wished she knew she didn't have to be afraid of his dog. She rested her hand on her lap, uncertainty in her eyes.

Trent pulled his .45 from his waistband and held it close to his leg. He'd never had to use it on a camping trip, and never planned to, but if it came to self-defense, he wouldn't have a choice.

She gasped. "Are we safe here? If they find us, there's no place to run."

He pointed at Rex. "Stay and watch out for her." Brooke's evaluation of the situation was 100 percent correct. "I'm going to see where they're headed. He put his finger close to her lips. "Stay quiet and listen, okay?"

She nodded, and Trent eased away, taking long strides, ducked behind the tall brush and moved briskly behind a massive tree trunk closer to the trail. He had a good visual of the men. He pulled out his cell and snapped a picture.

"I'm tired of carrying this tent," one man said.

"You're the one who wanted it," another responded.

"Quit complaining. Dump it. But toss it where no one can see it from the trail," the man with the smooth voice said.

"Okay, okay. How about over there behind that rock?"

"Whatever."

Trent froze. *The first rock, please.* Another prayer? Steps rustled in the grass, and heavy breathing filled his ears. A clump. A cough.

"Hey, there's bear scat over here. Must be one close by." His steps rustling in the grass grew farther away. "Let's get moving before the thing appears and decides we're dinner."

"She's out here somewhere. Whoever's helping her

is gonna pay for getting involved. Keep your eyes and ears open for movement."

Cigarette smoke blew through the trees and into Trent's nostrils. His fists tightened.

Thunder rolled and lightning cracked the sky. The damp smell of rain filled the air. He had to get back to Brooke and Rex and find shelter before the storm hit. Rain and mud at the edge of the cliff could be deadly.

"Come on, Zeke. Quit nosing around. We've gotta get movin' or we'll get drenched."

"Want me to go back for the tent?"

"Good idea. We'll find an open spot and set it up. Better hurry. We'll spread out and search the area again after the storm passes. They're close. I can feel it."

The bearded guy jumped from the tall grass like a gazelle, scooped the tent into his arms and returned to the trail.

The men walked fast, pointing and talking about possible tent sites. Their voices faded with their distance. Trent ran to get Brooke and Rex.

"Snake." One man's voice echoed from a distance.

A shot fired.

Brooke startled, and Rex hopped up on all fours. Her wide eyes searched Trent's face. He took Rex's leash from her. Concern for her well-being tensed his muscles. No one should be in this situation, especially a pregnant lady who is going into labor. Trent looked over the cliff and across the ravine. The magnificent scenery no longer held its beauty. Only the obstacles and dangers bombarded his mind. How much more could he handle? Sweat dripped from his forehead.

"Can we stay here? I don't want to go anywhere."

She drew her legs up and wrapped her arms around them as best she could.

"You know we can't."

A tarantula crawled up from around the edge of the cliff. She pushed to her feet and danced in place. "Changed my mind."

"Not as bad as it looks." Trent pushed it aside with his foot, took her hand and helped her back around the rock.

"That's the biggest, most frightening spider I've ever seen." Her body shook as she brushed at her clothes.

Thunder rolled and a bolt of lightning split the sky. If only the guy had left the tent.

The wind swirled, tossing her ponytail. The strong, damp scent of rain hit his nostrils. He looked back. A wall of rain raced across the ravine toward them. No time to build a shelter. He retrieved the small tarp from his backpack and shook it open. With the forest all around, the only possible cover was the trees. He placed his arm around her shoulders and rushed her and Rex to an enormous tree trunk, pulled her close to his side and tossed the blue covering over their heads. Rex sat at his feet, between Brooke and him.

"You hold one corner and I'll hold the other. Hopefully, this will keep us from getting drenched." And hopefully, keep them all alive.

Chapter Five

Brooke leaned close to Trent's side while pouring rain pounded overhead. Her sense of security improved just being close to him. Something she hadn't felt in years. She caught herself staring at his lips and quickly averted her eyes. How could she find him attractive when Nick died last night, and she was about to have a baby her protector may have to deliver? She'd trusted Trent with her life, but could she trust herself to make wise decisions in their present situation?

His selfless acts of kindness had her shaking her head at the differences in personalities. Her husband had helped her when she insisted, but his focus was making it big someday and becoming rich. She supposed that was why he gambled so much, thinking she didn't know. How could she not know when he kept withdrawing money from their account?

If the situation were reversed, Nick would run for cover and leave her to find her own shelter. Not that he didn't care, she surmised, he just took care of number one, himself. She'd loved his enthusiasm and entrepreneurial nature until he started hanging out with "new friends" as he'd referred to them and she'd noticed changes in him, none positive. Disappointment loomed over her failed marriage and Nick's death.

"How are you holding up?" Trent broke her train of thought. There he was, being thoughtful and nice again when no one forced him.

"About as well as slamming the oven door when I'm baking a cake." She faked a smile and held her breath through another contraction.

"What? Is that a bad thing?" A smirk spread across his face and the sparkle in his eyes caught her off guard.

She grinned at his lack of baking knowledge. "Well, a cake will fall flat if you bump it while it's cooking."

"Interesting," he said. "So, that's why my mom always made me get out of the kitchen when she baked. I never asked why, but I kept watch for when she made the icing. She'd let me lick the beaters and scrape icing from the bowl."

Thunder growled so loud the ground shook. Another bolt of lightning popped and exploded close by, and her feet tingled in her shoes. She startled. A cracking sound filled her ears.

Rex hopped to his feet and whined.

Trent patted Rex's head. "It's okay, boy." He threw off the tarp. "We've gotta get out of here. Lightning struck a tree. Sounds like it split and may fall our direction with this wind."

"Where do we go? There are trees all around us." Rain pelted her face and soaked her clothes. Her protruding belly became more prominent.

He wrapped the tarp around her body, and she held it

in place. He clutched Rex's leash with one hand and took her free hand with the other. "We'll find another tree on the opposite side of the trail until this storm passes."

They trekked through miniature streams of rainwater rushing over pine needles as they flowed downhill. Larger puddles splashed more water and mud on her already wet maternity capris and soaked tennis shoes. She gripped the tarp tighter, her only shield from the rain. She wouldn't let go. *Hold on, little guy. At least you're sheltered.*

Her foot slid on the muddy trail. Trent helped her get her footing stabilized. Either the rain eased up or the thickness of the trees shielded her some from the downpour. He led her to another tree where several enormous rocks offered a place to sit. She handed him the tarp and sat on the wet surface. He sat beside her with Rex at his feet and covered their heads again with the blue plastic.

"Gotta hand it to you. For a city girl in your condition, you're handling the hike better than I'd expected."

"When someone kills your husband in cold blood and starts coming after you to take your baby, survival mode kicks in. All the nature shows on television make mountain life look fun and adventurous. I'm not convinced. While I frantically ran through the woods, my mind went haywire. I couldn't see anything in the pitch black. All I could do was pray I wasn't running into a bear's den. Running into you was a dream come true."

Rain tapped on the blue plastic and dripped around her feet. If only her parents knew of her dilemma. She pushed back tears as little thumps punched against her belly. Her aspirations of enjoying the last days of her pregnancy shattered.

"Want to feel Josiah kicking?" She took his hand and placed it on her abdomen.

Josiah kicked again and Trent's eyes lit up. A huge smile filled his face. "Unbelievable." Realization hit him. He couldn't, wouldn't let anything happen to this baby, but possible delivery still troubled him.

"I know." She pushed a strand of hair away from her eyes. "What's the likelihood of me finding a K-9 handler with his partner in the middle of the forest? Perfect timing, I'd say. By the way, I'll buy you a new tent when we get out of here."

"Forget it. I'd already decided to invest in a larger one when I got home. Think I'd outgrown that one. Either that or I started carrying too much gear."

She mulled over his kindness and determination to get her to safety. She'd make sure he received a huge tent as a gift for helping her and Josiah.

"Do you think we'll get out of here before I go into labor?" Her mind reeled at the what ifs. Fear of the unknown raced through her and her body ached relentlessly. She shuddered. "You still haven't answered my question about why you won't deliver my baby, and why were you out here alone, anyway? Don't people normally hike in twos or more?"

"A lot of people like hiking alone. It's nothing unusual. I have Rex, so I'm not alone."

"If I go into labor, you will help me, right?"

"Are you cold?" He slid his arm around her and pulled her closer.

"You just changed the subject again. I realize you

don't owe me anything, but we're hiding out in the forest together and I don't know what's going on with you. Would you, please, tell me?" She leaned away and stared at him.

Rex nosed his way between them.

He sucked in a breath. "Truth? My sergeant suggested I take a few days off to reset after going to the scene of an accident three weeks ago." He cleared his throat. "I found a pregnant woman thrown from her car. She went into labor and her preemie died in my arms." He looked away. "Losing that baby ripped a chunk out of me. I'm out here because camping helps me clear my mind and think better. Me delivering your baby can't happen. I don't want to ruin your life."

"But it wasn't your fault. You can't blame yourself." Her heart ached for his dilemma.

"Enough about me." He straightened. "I asked if you were cold."

"No. I'm sweating and thinking about what's happening." Thoughts of moving from his side dissolved. His warmth and caring melted her resistance. He'd just spilled his heartbreak. He needed consoling as much as she. It was nice being around someone who offered compassion and thought of her needs over his own. She scolded herself for feeling vulnerable. He dropped his arm and petted Rex.

"Hard to say how labor will progress. Braxton-Hicks can last for weeks. It's a possibility they're causing the pain. Then again, could be the real thing. The trail ahead isn't easy and could cause more undue strain on your body. If I have any choice in the matter, you won't give birth out here in the mountains."

"I don't intend to." She held her breath and fought the tightness closing in on her abdomen.

A twig snapped. She jerked her head and widened her eyes, looking to Trent for a response. She cringed and waited for a gunshot or for someone to grab her from behind.

Trent slowly stuck his head out from under the tarp, trying not to make any noise, then covered back up.

"It's a twelve-point buck," he whispered. "Take a look."

She eased the plastic away and stared at the stately creature standing under a tree in the distance. Free and wild. He turned his head toward her, then bounded away with his white tail in the air. She ducked her head back under the cover.

"That was incredible. I've only seen deer at the zoo and they're not that big."

"Your attitude about animals in the wild makes all the difference in how you see them. Take bears for instance. They are massive, powerful creatures, and can kill you in one swipe of their paw, and yet—"

"Like you said earlier, no disrespect, but I don't want to hear about how I could die right now." She shivered at the thought.

"No, seriously, in most cases, if we respect the wildlife, they'll respect us."

She had every intention of respecting and staying away from all the animals and creepy crawling things. "Just get me out of here."

He nodded and eased the plastic back. "It's barely sprinkling now. Better get a move on."

Someone sneezed, and her heart thudded. Rex looked up at Trent. The men hadn't gone far.

"Stay quiet," he told Rex. "Come on. We've got to get farther away from the trail." He folded the tarp as quietly as possible, draped it over his arm and took her hand. "Be as quiet as you can, okay?" His voice was barely audible.

She tiptoed and tried avoiding any visible twigs. His grip on her hand had her arm stretched out as far as it would go. His long, quick stride forced her to double-time her steps. She was tired of running and her muscles were sore, but she wasn't about to let go of his hand, her lifeline. She upped her pace and her tummy ached with every bounce.

He stopped in some thick bushes and laid the partially folded tarp on the ground, then pointed for her to sit. She didn't have to wait for instructions. The water didn't matter either; she'd do whatever he told her. She was out of her element and had no idea how to help herself, here in the forest. He took off his backpack, laid it in the grass and slid down beside her with his pistol drawn. Would the drumroll in her chest give them away?

The men's feet sloshed on the wet trail. They drew closer and closer.

Rex jumped to his feet. The hair on the back of his neck raised along with a deep guttural sound.

Trent patted Rex on the head. "Quiet. Down." Rex lay down next to Brooke. His ears stood tall.

"Once we nab her, how do you want to play this out?" The gruff voice turned her stomach.

"Take her back to that abandoned cabin," the man

with the smooth voice said. "I'll keep her there while you two go back and get the four-wheelers. The doc is on standby. We'll take her to his place until the kid comes."

"You gonna shoot her after that?" The third guy chimed in.

"Nah, the doc will give her a shot. She'll go to sleep and never wake up."

Brooke held her breath. She dared not move or cause her clothes to rake across the plastic tarp and make a noise. If they caught her, she'd fight to the end. It wasn't Trent's responsibility to protect her. She'd caused her own dilemma by coming to the mountains. Proof she couldn't trust herself and shouldn't trust anyone else.

The guys moved on at a slow pace checking both sides of the trail. Once they were a distance away, Trent raised up, then stood. "We'll have to take a different route. This one's too dangerous with them running back and forth. They know you're not too far away and could double back any time." He helped her to her feet, grabbed his pack and tossed it on his back.

"Do you know where we are?" She tugged at her soaked clothes, wiped perspiration from her brow and picked up her walking stick. Her wet ponytail slapped her cheeks. She longed for a shower and clean clothes. None of her friends would believe she'd stepped one foot in the mountains, much less gone hiking. The cool rain sent a shiver over her body.

"I have a compass." He paused. "Careful, there's a hole."

"And you know where we're going?"

"As long as we continue north, we're headed in the right direction. Trust me."

She looked at him with uncertainty. She didn't trust him, and that was as scary as her situation.

Trent chewed his lip, debating on the best route to take to avoid her pursuers. Getting off course could take longer, and he'd risk the trail forcing her into hard labor. But then, following Redbud Trail put her at high risk, too. He fought the anger building inside him and focused on his determination to protect her. The likelihood of delivering her baby seemed unavoidable. His insides churned.

A quick glance in her direction reminded him of how she fit perfectly by his side. Why did he have to meet her like this, nine months pregnant, right here, right now? He didn't want to risk complications with birth, and he didn't want to lose her. She'd piqued his interest and his longing to be with her grew stronger.

Rex stood, wagging his tail. His big dark eyes watched his every move. Trent wiped his face with his free hand and continued through the tall grass. His insides churned and doubts of them reaching the ranger station before delivery loomed. He told her to trust him. How ironic when he hadn't trusted his own instincts for weeks. He'd thought CPR would put breath in the preemie's lungs, but he couldn't have been more wrong. Proof he wasn't the one in control.

He dropped her hand and dug in his pants pocket for the compass. Northwest. He adjusted his stance to the north and studied the terrain. Not a trail in sight. If he remained parallel to the main path, how far off track could they get? He'd have to pay attention and not get off course.

"Keep your eyes open. We're going to maintain a safe distance from the trail. It's not my first choice, but our lives may depend on it."

"As long as you know what you're doing."

He looked back at her. She stared up at the trees. Was she praying? Her hands rubbed circles over her belly, but she wasn't wearing a grimace. No contraction. He'd do his best to save her and Josiah, and help her overcome her fears of nature. That he could do, but it didn't mean he had to like what the next few hours might hold.

The fluff in her hair, gone. Rain made sure of that. No signs of any makeup. He imagined her as a businessperson who kept herself polished and never left home with a hair out of place. But she was absolutely beautiful right now.

"My eyes and ears are more open than they've ever been. I could probably hear a butterfly fluttering right now." She licked her lips. "I can handle level ground, but rocks and tree roots mess with my balance. I need a drink of water."

"Sure." He handed her the water bottle she'd asked him to hold. She took a couple of swallows and handed it back. He gave Rex a treat.

"Thanks. I'm ready now."

"Watch your step." He went around several large copses and some rocks taller than his house, with her a short distance behind. He ignored the rumbling in his stomach. Finding edible berries like wild strawberries or red elderberries would suffice if he spotted any. Problem was, wildlife ate berries, too, especially bears.

They traipsed through the wet, uneven terrain. Vines and tall weeds caught on his jeans. Several prickly thorns scraped his arms. Rex jumped over the small bushes and pranced around, sniffing.

Trent paused and checked on Brooke. The thorns were pulling at her clothes, but she hadn't complained. Should he rethink their direction?

"This wasn't the best choice. Maybe we should have walked the trail and taken our chances."

She caught up with him and tugged at the oversize shirt she still wore. His heart sank when he spotted tiny spots of blood seeping through the sleeves. Had they pricked her belly as well? Definitely, a bad choice. He raked fingers through his hair. Rex trotted back and stood, staring up at him.

"Looks like we're almost through this briar patch." She leaned her walking stick against a tree, pulled the scrunchie from her hair and finger combed it and pulled it back into a ponytail. "They'd never believe we came this direction. I say we keep going, unless you have a better plan."

He lifted his eyebrows and studied her. She hadn't complained and had forced herself to keep moving. Tougher than he thought. He checked his compass again.

"If you can handle it, we'll keep going. I see an opening up ahead."

"I've made it this far." Her eyes brightened and met with his. "I've got full confidence in you." What happened to the fearful city-girl persona? Was she having a change of opinion?

"Okay. Let's do this." He turned back around. Full

confidence? Uneasiness crept up his spine. He proceeded toward the opening.

Rex stuck his nose in the air and led the way.

Her walking stick bumped his leg a couple of times, so he knew she was close behind him. "There's a dip right here. Watch your step."

"How long have you been coming to the Smokies?"

"Six years. Started out with a group of friends. Guess I've walked most of these trails. Some lead over the northern section at the outer edge of where the Smokies meet up with Chilhowee. The main incline started back there at the Redbud Trail sign where we entered the Great Smoky Mountain National Park. There's some beautiful scenery with the upward climb just waiting to be discovered."

He emerged from the thicket and stopped. A flowing stream blocked their path. Rex lapped a drink. Brooke stepped beside him. He looked at her protruding belly and winced.

"What's wrong?" She glanced down at her abdomen, then back up at him.

"We need to cross the water. Looks shallow." He calculated about twenty feet to the other side. No way to judge the clear, rushing water's depth. "I'll go first and check it out." Brooke and Josiah's safety concerned him.

She placed her hands at her sides and stretched. "Another first for me. Are you sure it's safe?"

"*Sure* and *safe* don't belong in the same sentence when it comes to hiking or being thirty-eight weeks pregnant, on the verge of delivery and crossing a flowing river." He popped his neck. "Once Rex and I cross, I'll come back and help you."

She chewed on her lip. "Whatever you think."

He stepped into the icy water. Rex jumped in and bounced ahead. Trent steadied himself and tried making the task look easy. Rushing water pushed against his legs, casting more apprehension for Brooke's safety. Her falling could cause more problems and delays in their progress.

The cold water rushed inside his hiking boots, freezing his toes. He sucked in a breath and kept moving. Midway, the water grew deeper and struck him just above his knees. He looked back, forced a smile and waved at her. In an instant, his foot slipped out from under him, and he plummeted underwater. He floundered to his feet. Rex barked and rushed to his aid, gripped his pants leg with his teeth and tugged. "I'm okay," he whispered. "Thank you for helping me."

Rex bounced back to the shore and shook water from his fur.

Trent wiped his face with wet fingers. Embarrassment replaced the shiver from the cold water and wet clothes. So much for his tough-guy persona. The guy who did search and rescue for a living. Frustration edged with humiliation.

"Are you okay? Trent, are you okay?" Brooke's voice seeped into his water-filled ears.

"Yes. I slipped."

"Oh no." She rubbed circles on her belly. *"Hope I don't slip on those slick rocks."*

He proceeded to the other side and faced her. She stood across the river, with her hands folded under her chin. Was she praying? Maybe he should too.

"I'll come back and help you across." He pulled his

wet shirt away from his body and squeezed. Water trickled to the ground and a little chill rushed over him as a slight breeze blew under the shade of the trees. He shifted to a small area where the sun warmed his body.

"Meet me half-way. I think I can at least get that far."

"Are you sure?" That would be the point where he fell in.

She eased into the water with her hands stretched out to each side like walking a balance beam. Concern for her had him retracing his steps fast and bypassing the danger point. He couldn't risk letting her fall.

He reached for her and grabbed her hand, then her elbow, then held her around the waist as best he could. A tinge of satisfaction rushed over him, holding her. It felt right.

"Thank you for your help. I was a little nervous, well, honestly, I was really apprehensive." She gripped one of his hands that rested on her waist.

They inched their way to the other side. He helped her onto dry ground. Her wet ponytail swiped his face. His heart rate increased.

"Oh, I didn't mean to do that." With a quick turn of her head, her nose almost bumped his.

He held her gaze. "No problem." Thoughts of trying out her rosy lips crossed his mind, but now wasn't the time. He backed away.

Rex met her at the edge of the water and sniffed her feet and legs.

She raked her fingers through her wet ponytail and fluffed it, then wiped her face again. "Do you have a mirror?"

"Do I look like someone who'd carry a mirror on a camping trip?" he asked with a smile.

"Uh, no. Didn't hurt to ask."

Rex's ears straightened, then lay back. A throaty growl sounded. Trent spun at the rustling of the tall grass. A bear cub emerged. The hair on the back of his neck bristled.

Trent pulled the leash close and grabbed Brooke's hand. "Run. We've gotta get out of here."

"I don't like that word. You're scaring me."

He squeezed her hand and traipsed uphill, pulling her at a fast pace. The sow hadn't made her appearance, but where there was a cub, the mother was close by. His pulse raced through his body as if he'd sucked down a case of energy drinks.

"Trent. What is it?" She huffed breathlessly. "I… I can't keep this pace."

He gripped tighter and pulled harder until they reached the top of the incline. He slowed and trudged forward until the stream disappeared at the base of the mountain. He helped her a few more steps until she abruptly stopped and held her belly.

Rex stood, watching behind them. He stiffened with his ears going back and forth, up and down, staring down the mountain. Trent's focus shot back toward the stream. Sure enough, the sow joined her two cubs and stood in the middle of the water.

"That was close. Are you okay? We'd be mincemeat if we'd stuck around another minute." He checked his watch. "It's been an hour since your last contraction. That's good. I know I'm pushing you and you're tired, but we've got to keep moving. The more distance we put between us and that mama bear, the better."

Brooke held her belly and looked back. "What a magnificent scene. She's protecting her babies, like I'm trying to protect mine." She blew out a long breath, turned back to him and stretched her arm out. "If we're going up that incline, I need an elevator. Could you arrange that for me?"

"If you're willing to wait while I place the order." Her attempt at humor warmed him. "How about a tow instead?"

"I would if I could." He lengthened the leash again and gripped Brooke's soft hand. They trudged forward. Up and up. His wet clothes cooled him in the August heat. Brooke's cheeks reddened, and perspiration rolled down her face.

His stress level had skyrocketed. Too close for comfort. He'd spotted some wild berries before the cub appeared. Should have known a bear would treat her babies to the tasty fruit. Who knew just how close they came to an attack?

His legs burned, and if they rebelled at the incline, he wasn't sure how she kept going. She hadn't complained, but her huffing said it all. He stopped at a small clearing.

"Oh, thank you. I'm about to collapse. My legs are so wobbly, and I ache all over. Mountain climbing through the thicket, crossing a stream and running uphill differs greatly from hiking the trail and its gradual incline." She wiped her forehead. "Any idea where we are? My back aches something fierce."

He retrieved his compass. "We're still headed north. Well, a little northeast." He surveyed the area and pointed. "The hiking trail isn't far. We'll head that way for a reprieve."

"Sounds good to me. Maybe those guys gave up and are long gone." She rubbed her thighs.

"Ready?"

"Like baking in an oven when it hasn't preheated."

He pondered her comment a moment before he understood. Her baking comments only showed her passion for the profession she'd chosen. He loved his job as a K-9 handler and found pleasure talking about it under normal circumstances. There was nothing normal about it now, and being with Brooke in her condition only heightened his discomfort.

The sky darkened for the second time. He blew out a frustrated breath and pointed to a fallen tree. Sprinkles tapped his head and shoulders.

"Head over there. We can sit a minute until this shower passes."

"I am beyond exhausted." She rubbed her face. "Just when I think I can't take another step, you push me farther. I'm ready to drop."

He retrieved the damp tarp from his bag and sat beside her, tossing the thin blue plastic over their heads again. Who knew this waterproof material would become a shelter?

Rex hopped up and sat beside him. The thickness of the trees formed a canopy over them and shielded them from the brunt of the downpour.

She held one corner of the plastic that draped over her shoulder. "What kind of tarp is this anyway? My dad has a large one, but it's much thicker."

"It's called an ultralight tarp. Makes it easy to store in my backpack." He drew his feet closer to the tree.

"Have you always worked with canines?" Her question caught him off guard.

"I've always loved animals, dogs especially. My uncle was a cop, and I admired his commitment to serve and protect. He's the one who suggested I apply with the police department and work toward joining the K-9 specialty unit."

"Did that take a long time?"

"Once I secured the job as a police officer, it took over four years for me to prove myself a trustworthy officer who only needed minimal supervision. I went through all the required training, and here I am."

"That's outstanding." She brushed grass from the knees of her pants. "As a teenager, I did a lot of baby-sitting to raise money for my baking supplies. I've always loved children and baking. It was, and still is, fun to bake and watch smiles appear on customers' faces when they bite into a sweet treat. I still bake cookies for the neighborhood kids every chance I get."

"I'm sure the smell of cookies baking had them lined up at your door."

"You know it." She rubbed her belly. "It amazes me how quickly I fell in love with Josiah, and I haven't even met him. He means the world to me. Who knows, he may become a chef or a K-9 handler like you." She grew quiet. "I never dreamed I'd end up a single mom."

Discussing her husband's murder wasn't a subject he wanted to address again. Not now. She was tense enough. Delving into a replay of the scene would only stir more grief. She'd have plenty of questions to answer once they reached the authorities. Keeping her focused was hard enough. "Have you figured out the identity of the third guy or where you've heard his voice?"

"It's bizarre. My mind goes blank every time I think about it. And the times they've been close enough to get a visual, you've had me duck. I might recognize him if I see him."

"If we run across them again, maybe you can catch a quick glance. Like I said before, Rex and I could take them on, but it isn't in your best interest. You're in no condition to fight should something go wrong. If they find us and incapacitate me and abduct you like the man said, wait until the other two guys leave and the one with you falls asleep before you attempt escaping again."

"That's not going to happen." She bowed up.

He reached over and squeezed her hand. She cut her watery eyes up at him. He spoke slow and precise. "I'm saying if they overpower us and don't kill me, I'll find you." He patted his pistol. "And I'll do whatever's necessary to save you and your baby." Being with Brooke, Trent noted, the anxieties that plagued him since the accident hadn't materialized. He still faced the dreaded task, but a sense of strength welled up inside him. He liked the confidence she instilled in him.

Chapter Six

Brooke's insides trembled at the thought of those men catching up with her and what they might do to Trent. She refused to think about it.

"Tell me about your bakery."

Smart guy redirecting her miserable thoughts to a more pleasant subject.

"It has a simple name. Brooke's Bakery and Pastries. I dreamed of having my own business for years, so when this little shop went up for sale, I took the plunge and bought it. Hired a couple of exceptional employees. On opening day, we filled the display cases with cookies, cupcakes, petit fours, cakes and pies. I sold everything except for two strawberry cookies and a blueberry pie."

"You lost me at petit, what?" He had a way about him that calmed her.

"They're small bite-sized confectionery and tasty appetizers." She showed him the approximate size with her fingers. "You'd like it. Most have delicious icing covering them."

"Hmm, now that sounds good. Maybe I can stop by your shop and try one someday."

"I'll make you as many as you want when we get out of this jungle."

The wind whipped around and jerked the tarp from her grip. "Oh, no."

"I've got it." He readjusted the cover. "Summer is a prime time for thunderstorms. It's kinda like baking. The mountain-heated air rises and meets with the atmosphere and bakes up a storm."

"I like your analogy." She bounced her wet tennis shoes against the tree trunk and knocked mud off. "Makes sense." Her toes squished inside her socks.

She peeked from under the tarp. Clouds moved swiftly across the sky and the sun popped through, leaving them to deal with the slick terrain and the heat. Trent stood, shook water from the plastic and folded it to the size of a piece of legal paper. He stuffed it back inside the small case and shoved it into his bag, then pulled out some snacks, and held out his hand.

"The menu today is energy bar, peanut butter crackers or beef jerky. None of it has icing on it. Take your pick."

"Think I'll try the energy bar. Maybe it will help me move faster." She tore the package open and took a bite. Tasted like medicine, but who was she to complain? He handed her the leftover bottled water she had earlier.

Rex hopped off the log and wagged his tail. He smelled food.

"Here." Trent gave him a meal replacement bar and poured a little water in his bowl. Rex gobbled it down and lapped up every drop of water. "You were hungry, weren't you?" He patted the dog's furry sides.

"What's your favorite meal or restaurant?" She studied his unkempt hair and heavily shadowed beard. Some woman should've already snagged him up.

"Steak, of course. What man doesn't like a good medium-well steak with a loaded baked potato dripping in butter and sour cream, and a huge glass of sweet tea?" He licked his lips.

"Could've guessed." She tucked a stray strand of hair behind her ear. "We'll have to celebrate our rescue when we get out of here."

His gaze made her reevaluate what she'd said. "It's a date." He squared his shoulders and lifted his eyebrows.

A date? That wasn't what she meant. Heat rushed to her face. A celebration, that's all. Could he see her blushing? She couldn't think about a relationship right now. Friendship, maybe. She had to have her baby and bury her husband. Too much emotion to deal with. Besides, uncertainty still loomed over her own trust issues. Could she even make a good decision?

His bright eyes turned serious. "We've been walking around the hilly mountain valley to avoid the altitude, but to get back to the ranger's station we have to turn toward the main hiking trail." He looked into the distance, then back at her. "I won't lie, but after this rain Redbud trail is slick and dangerous. It spirals upward and around the side of the mountain. Once we're at the top, it's downhill the rest of the way."

"Then we'll have to take it slow." Staying alive and saving her baby were top priority. One step at a time and one foot in front of the other.

The serious look on his face had her biting her lip. She'd stay put and wait for help if anyone knew where to search. Her parents were most likely hysterical by now. No one at work would miss her until Monday, when she didn't show up at the bakery.

If anyone discovered Nick's body and found her purse and word of his death made it to the news stations, authorities were probably blaming her for his murder, unless they'd found footprints of the three men. With no access to the internet or television, there was no way to know what news went out over the air waves and no way to let her family know where to find her.

She took the last bite of the energy bar and emptied the water bottle. Trent stuffed the empty bottle and trash from the bars into a side zipper in his bag. "We'll need to refill these bottles when we run across another spring."

Josiah kicked her side. She rubbed her belly and blew out a breath. Spring water? Did they need to boil it first? "I've been so scatterbrained that I don't remember what we did with our walking sticks."

"Dropped mine when we ran from the bear cub. Hang tight—I'll get us another one." He walked away.

"Are you sure I'm safe here alone?"

"On second thought, I'll grab a couple on our way to the trail." He reached for her hand. "Ready to go?"

"I'm as ready as I can be, considering."

Her feet throbbed and her back ached. At times, her head spun. She'd purposely tried carrying on a conversation to keep from dwelling on her dilemma. Anything to change the subject and keep her mind off her surroundings.

Trusting a total stranger stressed her, and to think, she'd put her and Josiah's lives in his hands. He was a cop and so far, he'd proven resourceful, truthful, and, well, helpful and understanding. Not to mention, his good looks. Maybe those positive traits came from his desire to help people.

He stepped over the tall grass with ease. Her arm grew sore from all the pulling. He halted. "I knew we couldn't be too far from the path." His eyes sparkled from the sun filtering through the trees. He didn't deserve the imposition she'd placed on him. If it wasn't for her slow pace, he could've been home by now.

He scooped up two branches and cut the twigs away with his pocketknife. "Here you go." He handed her the wet walking stick. "Ready?"

"Like cake batter waiting to go into the oven." Not that ready, but they had to keep going. A pain hit, and she bent double. "Oh, oh, this…this one's different. Harder."

He stepped beside her and held her arm. "Careful not to fall over. It's been about forty-eight minutes since the last one. How is this one different? Tighter, stronger, more pressure, what?"

Rex stood by Trent, staring. His head tilted like he wanted to understand.

"Extremely tight." She straightened and rubbed her low back with her free hand. "Oh, my, I don't want to have another one of those."

"Sounds like the real thing, just not regular yet."

"Whew! Don't remind me."

"Point taken. Can you keep going?"

"I think so." *No, I can't. Everything aches.* If she admitted weakness, she'd collapse.

"Careful." He held her arm and helped her steady herself over the uneven ground.

She plodded through the thicket to the hiking trail. His hand dropped. The once dusty path looked perfect for a mudslide. Her lightweight, wet tennis shoes slid in the squishy substance.

"I don't mean to slow you down." She held her belly with one hand and the stick in the other. "Do you think I'd be safer if I walked at the edge of the grass rather than in the mud?" She rubbed her forehead. Maybe if she ignored the dull headache tightening above her eyes, it would go away.

"Try it and see. I'll keep an eye out for snakes, but you do the same."

"Ugh. Forgot about those." Chills raced across her shoulders. She'd rather ignore the possibility of one lurking. If only she could get past the phobia stage, maybe she'd overcome other fears of the wilderness. Not bears.

Rex pranced ahead of Trent, sniffing, and marking his trail. His brown-and-black coat had transformed from smooth and shiny to matted and dull, thanks to the weather.

The grass made for better traction. Her shoes gripped the ground better. The uphill climb argued with her already sore thighs, and pain crept into every muscle. Her constant low back ache heightened her determination to close the distance between them and the ranger's station.

"We're almost at the top this little path. Then we'll hit a slower incline that's less difficult and wider, and it starts winding around the side of the mountain. I'm sure it's muddy, but easier walking. Not many weeds or grass. A lot of protruding tree roots make perfect steps." He stopped. "Want my hand to help pull you up?"

"Please."

His firm grip offered the confidence she needed to make the last few steps. She looked back, surprised she'd endured the climb. Her head spun for a moment. She blinked a few times and the feeling disappeared.

A sense of relief swept over her as she stepped out of the tall grass. He'd described the trail before them accurately. Wide, clear of grass, but rocky, filled with scattered tree roots and muddy. Definitely, muddy.

A gradual tightening in her abdomen returned and the pain caught her breath. She hugged her belly and doubled over just as a loud pop rang out and the zing of a bullet broke the small tree limb by Trent's head.

Rex jerked at the leash, barking and growling.

Trent tugged Brooke and Rex out of sight from the bottom of the trail.

"Quiet," he told the German shepherd, who stopped barking.

Trent pulled his pistol and hunkered close to the ground, mentally kicking himself for putting them back in harm's way. Should've stayed out of sight. He rubbed the ache above his ear. Blood. The bullet grazed his head. A whole new meaning of *survival* kicked in.

"There they are. Got a dog with them." The men picked up their pace and gained ground.

Trent's thoughts went into overdrive. He could shoot one of them, but they'd fire back and could hit Brooke.

Small tree limbs and weeds lining the trail wouldn't shield them from flying bullets.

He wrapped his arm around her waist and semi carried her around the mountain's upward winding path farther away from their pursuers. How long would it take the men to catch up with them? His hiking boots held to the mud okay. But her tennis shoes were like ice skates, slipping with every step. His heart thumped like a jackhammer against his chest.

With the wall of the mountain on one side and a steep, angled drop-off by a river on the other, they had no other choice but to try to outrun the men. He'd traveled this path many times. There were no hiding places for three-quarters of a mile, just a simple winding trail. Only now it wasn't so simple. Brooke's last contraction was a mere fifteen minutes from the previous. How could he get her to safety on the slippery trail, keep them both alive and deliver a baby—who'd quickly start crying?

"I don't know how much farther I can go." Her head dropped. "My back is killing me, and I feel dizzy."

"You can do this. Focus on getting to the top of this mountain where we can call for help." They were a long way from the top, but he wasn't about to instill more fear and discouragement. About four more miles.

"Can you see them?" She looked up at him and gasped. "You're bleeding."

"It's nothing. No, I can't see them. The way we're moving in a circular pattern up the side of the mountain will make their visibility difficult as long as we don't stop."

"Did a limb do that, or did the bullet hit you?" She

bent over and clung to her tummy again. "I need a second."

"We don't have a second, but okay." He helped her sit on a large rock beside the mountain wall. "Stay here. I'm going to see where they are." He handed her Rex's leash.

Rex paced, then stopped. His head high and ears tall.

Trent backtracked and peered around the path and to the trail below. In the distance, the three men were gaining ground and closing in fast. Trent rushed back and found Brooke standing, waiting for him.

"I'm ready. I'm hurting, but I'm not about to let these creeps get their hands on my baby." She faced the winding trail and then looked at him and held her hand out.

He wrapped his fingers around her hand and trekked beside her up the trail. Her foot slipped several times, but she didn't falter. There was a new resolve about her. Was it her faith or her determination to save her baby? Didn't matter.

"You're doing great. I admire your newfound confidence. You've been a trouper through this horrific ordeal. We'll get through it together."

She pressed her lips together. Was it a smile or a grimace? He glanced at the sun through the overhang of mountain and trees. *A miracle would be good about now.* The familiar sound of a waterfall roared in the distance. Maybe the noise would muffle any screams or moans Brooke might make next time a pain hit. His next dilemma added more stress to their tense situation. There was no place to go but up the trail or off the side of the cliff. If the men caught up with them, there'd be a showdown for sure.

"What's that noise?" Brooke gripped his hand tighter.

"A waterfall. Have you ever seen one?" The last thing he wanted to talk about was a waterfall, but if the change in subject helped her cope, then so be it.

"In movies and on nature shows, but not in person. Will we have to go under it?"

"No. You'll be able to see it in a few minutes." He focused on the condition of the ground. "Watch your step up here. There are more tree roots. It might be easier for you versus the mud."

"I need easier."

The waterfall's roar grew louder the closer they got. Trent looked back. No signs of the men, but that didn't mean anything. Any one of them could pop around the bend at any moment. *Keep moving.*

"Aww, look. I see the waterfall." She let go of his hand and stopped. "It's magnificent and powerful. Loud, too. I can feel the cool mist coming from it."

"We've got to keep moving." He reached for her hand, but she stepped closer to the edge of the trail. "Don't go any farther." His breath hitched.

"Just another sec—" Her foot slipped, and she landed on her backside and slid off the side of the steep slope, out of sight.

"No!"

Rex lunged for the edge of the cliff. Trent unleashed him and Rex took off after her.

He shoved the leash in his pants pocket and hopped over the edge, grabbing at every tree trunk and root he could to slow his descent. His chest tightened and his mouth went dry. He couldn't get to her fast enough. Was she hurt? Did she land on Josiah? What about Rex?

Was he okay? No one could fall this distance and not get hurt.

His legs and arms scraped against tree roots and small rocks. The pack tugged at his shoulders but shielded his back from injury. His feet dug into the wet ground and mud and leaves flew over his head. Suddenly, he was airborne. He plunked to the bottom of the ravine, onto the sandy, rocky ground.

The sudden stop knocked the air out of him. He lay there breathless until the intense pain subsided. His dirty, bloody hand slapped over his chest and he sat up, sucking breath in slowly through his mouth and exhaling.

Rex ran to him and licked his face. He barked and ran a short distance from Trent, turned and barked again. The waterfall drowned out some of the noise. He pushed to his feet and staggered. "I'm coming. Go ahead. Search." He commanded.

Rex took off running. He followed him up under the overhang of tree roots and dirt. How did they land this far apart? He guessed grabbing trees on the way down shifted his direction.

His heart skipped a beat. Brooke lay on the sandy riverbank, inches from a large boulder. He raced to her side and fell to his knees. Had she hit the rock and bounced off?

"Brooke. Brooke. Are you okay? Answer me. What hurts?" He brushed hair from her face. The pink scrunchy tangled in her leaf-and-grass-filled hair. "Did you land on your belly?"

Rex sniffed, moved her hand with his nose, and sniffed her abdomen.

She moaned and tried lifting herself on her elbows, then lay back down. "I... I don't know. What happened?"

"You slid down the ravine."

She rolled to her side, and he helped her sit up. The back of her shirt had ripped, and blood seeped through.

"Talk to me." Adrenaline shot through him like an injection of caffeine.

She held out her bloody hands and rolled her shoulders. "I think I caught every tree root and thorn bush on the way down." Her weary eyes lifted and looked into his. "How did you and Rex get here so fast?"

Concern in those blue eyes caught him off guard. She'd slid down a good fifty feet and should be in pain, but here she sat asking about him.

"Rex chased behind you, and I followed him, but that wasn't part of our escape plan."

"Why did you follow me? You could've gotten hurt. Are you okay?"

She reached her hand out to Rex. He sniffed it. "Thank you, Rex. You are a faithful friend." She looked back at Trent. "Are you hurt? You never told me what made your head bleed."

"I'm fine. Do you hurt anywhere? Arms, legs?" He felt her pulse, the gently pressed around her belly. "Does any of that hurt? Did you hit your head?"

"No. No, I'm okay, I think. Just can't believe I fell." She rubbed her belly. "It's okay Josiah, mama didn't land on you."

"You've got some cuts on your back I need to check."

"Probably why it's stinging. I need to see if I can stand."

"No. Not yet. You've had enough trauma for today. Sit still." He hopped to his feet. "Let me get my first aid kit. Need to look at your hand, too." His hands were burned, his shirt torn, and a pile-up of mud on his pants. He dropped his bag on the ground and brushed away the collection of grass, leaves and mud caught on the buckles, zipper and strap clips.

He rushed over to the river and rinsed the blood and debris from his hands. Then grabbed a water bottle and returned to her. He lifted the back of her shirt and poured a small amount over her back. How had she escaped deep lacerations? Minor scrapes. He wiped them with an alcohol wipe and dug the antiseptic cream from the kit. "We don't have enough Band-Aids for every cut."

"Whoa, that burns." She stiffened. "It's okay—I don't need Band-Aids."

He dabbed the cream on her back, pulled her torn shirt down and looked at her hands. "There's a thorn in this hand and a few scrapes on both, but for the most part, your hands look good." He took the tweezers, pulled out the thorn and cleaned her skin with an alcohol wipe. "That will probably get sore. Do you want a Band-Aid on your hand?"

"No. We might need those later. Will you help me up?"

She held out her hand, but he leaned over and caught her by the waist and lifted her to her feet. Her hands went straight to her abdomen, and she huffed several breaths.

"I've got a lot of pressure." Her eyes widened and tears pooled. "I can't keep going." She pulled the ponytail holder from her hair, bent over and shook her head. Leaves and grass fell. A small green vine dangled. She tossed it away, then finger-combed her hair back into a ponytail.

Trent took in a deep breath, raked his stinging fingers across his face and faked a smile. "We'll rest for a while. As long as those guys don't find us, we should be okay. They won't expect us to jump off the cliff. Besides, they can't see us under this overhang. We'll keep moving as soon as you're ready."

His gut wrenched. He was very likely going to deliver this baby—maybe even today. Didn't look like they'd be going anywhere, anytime soon. He'd been trying to prepare himself, just in case. He popped the lid of an energy drink and took a gulp. Did it also pack a punch of confidence?

"I definitely cannot go any farther. But how are we going to have a baby out here with no help or supplies? You're going to have to deliver this baby. I can't do it without you. I have faith in you and God will help us both. He has to. I'm just as scared as you are."

"We'll make do. You'd better pray. God doesn't hear my prayers." He'd heard her declaration. She wasn't moving. And as much as he didn't want to admit it, time had come for him to get his emergency medical training in check and prepare for the inevitable.

Chapter Seven

"Tell me this isn't really happening. I'm not having my baby out here in the wilderness. I'm not." Maybe if Brooke declared it enough, she'd wake up from this nightmare. Trent was fully capable for the task, but his jutted jaw revealed his stress, which increased her own stress and made the pains worse.

The splashing roar of the waterfall drowned out all noises except for Trent when he stood close. Her mishap landed her close to the waterfall. Its fine mist cooled her sweaty skin. Boulders and fallen branches created an obstacle course on the opposite bank, while some large rocks protruded from the clear blue water. If she weren't in such a desperate situation, sitting by this scenic view might have been a romantic place to visit.

Trent spread out the still damp tarp for her to sit on, but a large log looked more appealing. Her body rebelled. She couldn't sit still.

"Stay here. I'm going around the bend to get an idea of where we are and gather some firewood. I'll build a fire under the overhang of the cliff wall so the smoke won't travel up. Those men have likely kept on the trail and are far from here now." Trent's long legs had him out of sight in an instant. Rex disappeared with him.

She'd help him, but how could she when she couldn't help herself? Was Josiah okay? Did the fall hurt him? Her lip quivered as tears rolled. The relentless pain in her back wouldn't quit, and the contractions intensified.

A moan spilled from her lips as another dreadful pain took her breath. She held her belly, trying to breathe like her instructor in Lamaze class taught. She didn't need a watch or Trent's timing. Contractions were coming nonstop. Fear surged in her gut. *Lord, You said to fear not because You are always with me, but I'm scared.*

The intensity eased. Nothing but trees. Would she recognize the trail if she saw it? Those men had shot at Trent. He never answered her question about the blood above his ear, but he didn't have to. Helplessness threatened. If they killed him, she'd never forgive herself, and she'd be in the hands of murderers.

"Ohhhhh." Her mouth flew open. She wrapped her arms around Josiah. Her eyes shot to the ground. A puddle of water formed around her feet.

Trent marched around the bend of the river, dragging something green. His face beamed until her eyes met with his eyes. "What is it? What's wrong?"

"My…water broke." Reality hit hard. "My water broke." Sobs erupted. She covered her face with both hands. No question about it, she'd have Josiah right here by the waterfall.

He dropped the object and scooped her into his arms. His firm embrace offered little comfort at the realization that they were alone in the forest, and she would give birth naturally. Not what she'd planned. She'd attended Lamaze classes to learn their breathing, relaxation and comfort techniques, but she'd fully intended to use medication for delivery.

"Everything will be okay. You're strong and determined. You can do this. We can do this."

She cried on his shoulder. His towering height and muscular embrace imparted a faint sense of security. The joy of finally holding her baby swept over her, but only for a moment. Worry stirred about potential complications.

She backed away and wiped her tears. "I'm scared."

"I can only imagine. But everything will be okay." He pointed. "Look what I found. Normally, it infuriates me when people litter the forest but right now this is a godsend."

She looked where he pointed and saw green material. "What do you mean?" She searched her thoughts. Godsend? Was the fall God's way of protecting her and Josiah from those pursuing her?

Rex drank from the river, moseyed over to a sandy spot, and lay down with his head high and ears up.

Trent retrieved the green fabric. "This," he said, shaking it, "is a tent. Has a rip in the top in a couple of places and ragged edges, but it has a floor. We can prop it up with a few tree limbs. You and Josiah will have shelter." He dragged it under the overhang.

Her delicate blue nursery at home rushed to the forefront of her mind. A dirty green tent wasn't exactly nursery decor, but it was better than nothing. Her eyes fell to Trent's waist. His pistols were still intact, strapped to his belt. A somber reminder that they weren't out of the woods yet, no pun intended.

"And for the record. Your fall may have been for the best." He tugged at the tent, spreading it out across the sand and rocky riverbank. "The men are long gone. They went on up the trail still tracking us, only we're not there." He gave her a thumbs-up and faked a smile as the realization hit hard. His pulse increased. If this birth went wrong, it would ruin him for life and destroy Brooke.

She bit back her disappointment and resolved to make the most of her situation. No amount of crying or arguing would change the fact that she was about to have her baby.

She leaned on a boulder at the edge of the water and watched Trent work hard to make her comfortable. He could have taken a chance and left her at the deserted cabin while he went for help. But no. He hadn't abandoned her.

Brooke let out a sigh. What would her life be like now? Alone? Just her and Josiah. She and Trent would surely go their separate ways once they were rescued.

The abrupt tightening around her entire abdomen almost knocked her off her feet. She moaned, rocked back and forth, and forced herself to breathe properly. Her legs weakened and her head hurt.

"I'm getting the tent up as fast as I can. Hold on." His tone was urgent and caring.

He tossed the small tarp away from the overhang and tugged the tent in its place, the perfect hideout. He took the four tree limbs and ducked inside the flattened tent. His head scraped the top until he pushed the limbs into the four corners, stepped out into the open and gave her a thumbs-up.

"Need one more to hold the center up." He traipsed back around the bend like a little boy on a mission and came right back. Her heart warmed.

"Should've brought this one, too. I'll see what I can do to make the floor presentable. Not much I can do with it though other than brush the leaves out. Oh, I can put the tarp on the floor. That will work. But I don't have tape to fix the rips in the roof. They aren't too big so maybe it won't be a problem."

"You're so resourceful. Where did you learn how to do all this?"

His ex-girlfriend made a bad choice when she left this guy. Why someone else hadn't snatched him up, she'd never know. "You're so smart and talented." She respected his efforts, all he'd done for her and all he'd have to do when he delivered the baby. "I can tell you pride yourself in helping others get through difficult situations, and you're good at it. You and Rex are a team, like you and I are the delivery team. We will get through this with God's help."

He ducked his head and disappeared inside the tent. Leaves and a few small rocks flew out of the doorway as he cleared the floor and spread the tarp out. Rex reclined nearby, watching. Trent stepped out and stretched his back, slapping dirt from his hands. He picked up his backpack, brushed dirt from it and tossed it inside the tent. "Come on in and check it out. You can help me sort things."

She held her belly and waddled inside. "Sort what

things?" She eased herself onto the damp, tarped floor. Her nose curled at the moldy dirt smell. Shelter, yes. Sterile, no.

He plopped on the floor beside her and opened his backpack. He handed her his extra pair of jeans and tennis shoes. "Making sure we have everything we need. Lay the jeans out like a table. We'll put delivery supplies on them. Take the shoestring out of one shoe and we'll cut it in half to tie off the umbilical cord."

She swallowed hard.

He placed an unopened bottle of water on the jeans and pulled small scissors from the first aid kit, placing them beside the string. "I'll build a fire and boil water from the river, sanitize my knife in case we need it. We have several small packets of alcohol wipes left, and of course, Mandy's baby blanket. When was the last time you saw your doctor?"

"Seeing all this makes me nervous and nauseous. I saw him Monday, why? Glad you know what you're doing."

"Did he indicate the position of the baby?" His eyes cut up at her.

"He said Josiah was head down and in position for delivery. And that I could go into labor any day."

Voices. She froze.

Rex started barking. The hair on the top of his back stood tall. Trent drew his weapon and peeked out of the tent. "Down, boy." Rex backed up but kept growling.

Trent waved his hand at her. "It's two guys. Not the bad ones." He slid his pistol back into the holster and stepped out into the open. She struggled to her feet, then followed behind him. The hikers, an older man and a younger one, gasped when she emerged.

The older man's eyebrows lifted, and his eyes went back and forth from Trent to her.

"My son wanted to get a closer look at the waterfall. Hope we're not disturbing you." He punched the teen on the shoulder. "See. I told ya. You never know where you'll find people in these mountains. About the time you think you're alone, someone appears. That's why you never shoot unless you have your target in sight."

He turned back to Trent. "Brought my kid on this trip to teach him the ins and outs of hiking, camping and hunting." He scratched his head. "Do you guys live around here? None of my business, but you look like you're in the wrong place."

"I *am* in the wrong place." Brooke brushed more dirt from her pants.

"Are you headed back to the ranger's station at Eagle's Point?" Trent interrupted.

"Yep, we've had more than our share of the forest for a while, but he insisted on a ground-level view of the falls. What about you?" The older man asked.

"We ran into some trouble a couple of miles back, and for obvious reasons we can't get to the station fast enough. I can't get a signal on my cell yet. Do you have a satellite phone?"

"No satellite phone and signal for us, either. My fault and another lesson learned. Thought I had it all together." The older man rubbed his chin. "He's going into withdrawals from his social media addiction." He patted the younger guy on the back. "Isn't that right? Is there anything we can do to help?"

Brooke straightened and faced the older man. "How soon will you reach the ranger's station?"

"My guess is sometime tomorrow afternoon."

Her hopes plummeted.

"As soon as you reach the ridge and have a signal, we'd appreciate you calling ahead and sending help," Trent said. "We'll do our best to stay near this trail, but my friend here is experiencing labor pains." He exchanged glances with Brooke.

"It's a long story," Brooke said. She placed her hand on her aching belly.

"Sure thing." The older man shuffled his feet. "What names do we give them?"

"Trent Williston, K9 officer." He reached out and shook the man's hand.

"Richard Hollingsworth, and, my son Dale."

Dale reached out to pet Rex, but Rex growled and showed his teeth.

"I wouldn't do that. Rex. Come." Trent hooked the leash on Rex's collar. "He's a police dog and very protective of me."

"I'm Brooke Chandler. I was supposed to have a quick trip to the mountains and back, but three men kicked our cabin door in and shot my husband. I ran through the forest until I met up with Trent. Now they're after both of us."

"Shot? On purpose?" Richard's expression changed as he looked around nervously. "We will report this as fast as we can." He grabbed his son's arm. "Come on, let's get out of here. Y'all hang tight. Help is on the way."

Trent and Brooke stood in silence as father and son

disappeared around the bend. Richard looked back several times. Did he believe them? Uncertainty swept over her. The whole scenario sounded farfetched. Who'd believe a pregnant woman would be bold enough to go hiking or camping at this stage of her pregnancy? And who would believe her husband had been murdered?

"Why are you looking at me like that?" Trent's eyebrows lowered.

"Richard didn't believe my story." Her heart sank. "They're running away to keep from getting involved."

"We can't judge them. Hikers are good to report problems to the rangers." He faced Brooke and held her shoulders. "It's important to keep a positive outlook, especially now." He bit back his words as doubts hammered at his confidence.

"If you say so." She held her belly. "A surge of expectation had me praying they had a phone and could call for help."

Rex growled and ran to the water's edge.

Bushes on the opposite side of the river rustled.

"Rex. Quiet. Come here." Rex backed away and returned to Trent's side.

"What is it?" Brooke gripped Trent's biceps. Her touch sent a charge through him.

"I don't see anything." He placed his hand on top of hers. "Don't worry—Rex will alert us if there's a problem."

Trent stepped back. His heel caught a protruding rock, and he fell backward, twisting his ankle and knocking the pistol from its clip.

Brooke picked up the weapon and held her hands in the air. "Go. Get out of here. Go. Now."

She dropped her shoulders and dangled the pistol on the trigger guard. "That was intense."

Trent retrieved the weapon and holstered it. "What are you doing?"

"I remembered what you did this morning with the bear, so I did it again. Did you hurt yourself?"

"But there was nothing there." He chuckled and brushed dirt from his pants. Prickly pains shot through his ankle. "Thanks for intervening, though. You've become more adapted to the wilderness than you realize."

"How was I supposed to know? The bushes shook. Could've been a bear hiding." She propped her hands at her sides. "Besides, you've taught me a lot in the short time we've been together.

Trent admired her innocence and yet, her strength. She had no idea how much he'd grown to like her, a lot. Another reason he dreaded the approaching task and the strain on his confidence.

Rex still stood facing the river, keeping a watchful eye across it. What would Trent do without his dog? Such a faithful canine.

"It's okay—we're not in danger unless a bear actually appears."

"Can we change the subject now?" She slid both hands under her belly and waddled back inside the tent.

He blew out a breath. She reacted the only way she knew and thought she was helping protect them. Brooke was smart and quick-thinking, and she didn't freak out or scream. She acted without hesitation. He chuckled under his breath. He liked her spunk.

Birds nearby sang their melody. The mist from the waterfall cooled his skin while he looked around for enough dry wood to make a fire. Nervous tension had him kicking rocks and tossing rotted limbs. He searched for signs of the trail above them. Hard to pin a location with all the trees. What path had Richard and Dale traveled to get down to the waterfall? He bit his lip. Should've asked.

Trent gathered some small branches and made his way back to the tent. Dusk threatened quicker than he'd imagined. The canopy of trees kept them shaded and cooler. What a day. He dropped the firewood and rolled his head in circles until his neck popped. He missed sleep last night keeping watch for the killers. Tonight wasn't looking promising. His mind wouldn't shut down. She depended on him, and he wanted to be there for her, but the nagging what-ifs kept him uptight. There was the potential of so many things going wrong in delivering a baby out in the environment, without proper medical supplies. A moan caught his attention.

"You okay in there?" He tossed the firewood on the ground and worked on building the fire mere feet from the tent's doorway.

"As okay as I can be," she moaned. "How are your head and your ankle?"

Her strained tone told him all he needed to know. He imagined her clenched jaw, barely holding on, and yet trying to remain strong and brave. Her bravery impressed him.

How was he supposed to deliver a baby in the dark? Who would hold the small flashlight in his pocket? An empty feeling hit the pit of his stomach.

"I'm good." The bullet scrape on his head burned. At least he was alive. An inch closer…he couldn't think about what the outcome would have been for himself and for Brooke and Josiah.

He busied himself retrieving his metal camping coffeepot and filling it with river water. Cleared a space for the fire, gathered several medium-sized rocks and formed a circle. Then broke the limbs and organized them where they wouldn't smother the blaze. He used the flame from his small propane tank to fire up some pine needles underneath the limbs. In a few minutes, the fire crackled, and flames danced. How long it would last with a mist in the air, he didn't know.

He set the water-filled coffeepot on the eye above the propane tank's flame.

"Can you hand me the knife? I left it beside the shoestring."

She shuffled from the tent and dropped the folded knife in his hand. "Do you think I'll make it until morning? How are we supposed to see in the dark? I mean, it's bad enough being in the middle of the mountains, but in the dark, too?"

"Let's take it one step at a time. Whatever happens, we'll face it together." Darkness fell over their camp faster than expected. He checked his watch, glad he'd invested in a waterproof, self-winding one made for outdoor activities. Eight thirty. Felt like midnight.

"We haven't eaten much today. What would you like?" One of his mom's delicious home-cooked meals would taste great. Mashed potatoes, white beans, cut corn, with her brown gravy, tender roast and rolls. Yum. His mouth watered at the thought.

"Guess an apple and one of those small trail mixes. What about you?"

"Beef jerky. I still have a partial energy drink. We're running low on water."

Rex eased over and curled up beside him. Trent emptied a bag of dry dog food in his bowl, and rubbed his soft fur. His tail flapped against the ground.

Brooke scooted to the edge of the tent and tossed the doorway flap aside. The reflection of the flames danced in her tired eyes. Poor woman hadn't stopped long enough to grieve her husband's death, and now she was facing another huge hurdle. He was, too. More than she knew. The battle raged inside him.

She bit into the apple. "I've made so many bad decisions. Meeting Nick at the cabin was the worst yet. Now, Josiah and I are paying for my lack of wisdom and I'm putting you through the trauma of dealing with your problem. If anything happens to Josiah, I'll never forgive myself."

"Exactly the reason I'm struggling with the delivery." Her words piled more apprehension on him. He'd never forgive himself either.

"I turned into a girlie girl after my frightening encounter. My goal in life, besides owning a bakery, was becoming the best wife and mother ever. I love doing all those wifely things."

"I'm sure you excel in anything you set your mind to." He had always excelled until the preemie's death.

"Funny, that's what my mom always said." Her half smile must have brought back a pleasant memory. "Are you afraid of anything?"

"That's a loaded question." He twirled a twig between his fingers. "Everyone has fears. What about you?"

"You already know my biggest fear. Just look around. I'm sitting in the middle of it." She swatted at mosquitos.

He stared into the fire. His mouth went dry.

"Well?" She dipped her head and turned it slightly.

He cleared his throat. "I've faced a lot of uncertainties. Thanks to Rex, I've never felt totally alone. We've searched some dangerous places for people who were lost, for missing children, lost seniors, armed criminals on the run and others. Out here I watch for wild hogs, mountain lions and coyotes, but right now my biggest—"

She hugged her belly. "Ugh. It hurts so bad." Her lips pressed together as she groaned.

He checked his watch. Still fifteen minutes apart and the first baby? Could be morning before she delivered. Wasn't unusual with the first child for labor to take hours, but not every woman fell fifty feet before delivery. Brooke differed from other pregnant women he'd encountered. They'd burst your eardrums, yelling with pain at the slightest onset of labor. She hadn't let out a single war cry, only moans.

A piercing scream, like that of a wailing child, sounded in the distance. It overpowered the waterfall's roar. Her head jerked up, her mouth flew open and her eyes widened.

"What was that? Is somebody hurt?"

"Mountain lion, I think. Could be a bobcat. I hear them often, but rarely see them. Don't worry—they eat deer and normally avoid people."

"You wouldn't lie to me, would you?" She rubbed circles on her belly. "I'm not cut out for this camping stuff."

"I'd never lie to you. I would let you know if we were in danger. Besides, I've watched you grow stronger and less fearful in the past few hours." He jumped up and kicked some rocks into the water. Pain hit his ankle.

She drew her feet as close to her body as possible. "You scared me. Now, what?"

"Scorpion." He slapped his palm to his forehead. Shouldn't have told her. Now she wouldn't sleep.

"Not funny. Do you have bug spray, or something that will keep them away?"

He sat back down and drew lines in the damp sand with a twig. "Not out here. If they were in your home, there are a few things a person can do to help get rid of them, but in the wild, it's pointless."

"Couldn't you just say it's gone or don't worry about them? I'm struggling to not freak out right now. Scorpions? Really?" She slapped at her shoulder. "Ugh. Thought something was crawling on me."

He searched her face and bit back a grin. Protecting her from the killers had become a dangerous challenge. Keeping her labor pains in check was another life-threatening event but watching her learn about nature and the dangers of hiking through the mountains added a little humor to those desperate situations. She was more in tune with her surroundings than she realized. Beautiful, too, even with her unkempt appearance.

"What time is it?" She yawned.

"Time for us to get some rest. Rex and I will guard the doorway while you sleep. I'm going to cut the tent's doorway flap off and we'll use it when you go into labor."

"You're so resourceful and smart. I'm certain there's nothing you can't do. I am so exhausted. Don't know if I can close my eyes, knowing there are scorpions and tarantulas around. Now that it's dark, I won't be able to see them." She shivered.

"Don't think about them. Think about holding your baby." *While I have nightmares about his arrival.*

"Easy for you to say. You're used to bugs."

She scooted back into the small tent while he cut the flap away and placed it inside. The open doorway, with the help of light from the fire, allowed him to monitor her. She lay on her side facing him and rested her head on her arm. He regretted not grabbing the blanket from his tent before they ran. Her eyes blinked a few times and closed. She moaned and tossed. Looked like she was in for a rough night, too.

He stared at the moon, glistening through the trees. What would morning bring? Harder labor pains? A baby? Her water broke earlier, which meant delivery would be within twenty-four hours or so. A baby would add to the delay of reaching the ranger's station and put more pressure on him to keep them safe.

He tightened his fists. The gnawing in his gut aggravated him. He knew how to deliver a baby, but what if something went wrong, again?

His thoughts drifted. If they didn't make it back home by tomorrow night, his parents would start calling the ranger's station. Since he'd always called them on his way home from these trips, they'd know something had happened if he hadn't made contact.

Brooke said she should have been home by this morning. Maybe her parents had already reported her missing and a search party was already out looking for them. Had she told her parents where she was going?

Regardless of whose parents responded and the time it took for search and rescue to find them, the baby would be here before anyone arrived. He'd be forced to face his fear.

Chapter Eight

Brooke curled up on the cool, hard ground and held her belly. Her body shivered. She slapped at every itch, praying an insect hadn't found her. She'd never dreamed of being in this predicament. Contractions kept her restless into the night. How much longer before Josiah's arrival? How much longer until morning?

The roar of the waterfall reminded her of the hum of a fan at her grandparents' house. The constant sound always lulled her to sleep on the pillow top mattress. It was cozy and warm, not like now, lying on the dirty floor of a ripped tent, becoming bait to any varmint lurking. Her imagination went wild and turned into a nightmare.

She bolted upright, sucking in the damp air. Chills of the night air swept over her. Blackness all around except for the fire outside the tent's doorway. Rex's head shot up and looked at her. He and Trent slept by the fire, and a small pile of limbs sat beside them. She'd seen him with the sticks earlier, but wondered if he'd left her alone at any point during the night. Her insides coiled with fear. She longed for home.

With no signs of daylight, she lay back down and stared at the crackling fire. *I'm worried. Keep us safe, please.*

Trent stirred. He dropped another small log on the fire and looked her direction. "You should be sleeping." His caring tone warmed her.

"How could you tell I was awake?"

"Your eyes are open." He lifted his arm and a small blue glow appeared on his wrist. "Three in the morning. We still have a couple more hours before sunrise. Rest as much as you can. How are the pains?" He unzipped the backpack and pulled out the jacket she'd worn last night, but returned it this morning when the sun warmed her up, and tossed it to her. "Should have thought of this sooner. I'm by the fire, but you must be cold with this mist from the waterfall and the lower night temperatures."

She sat up and slid her arms into the lightweight jacket. Why hadn't she thought to ask for it?

"Pains are about the same. They seem to have slowed, but I'm not sure. My entire body aches. Some of it is probably from the fall and from hiking." She rubbed her abdomen. "He hasn't moved since the fall. Makes me worry about him." Images of cradling Josiah in her arms warmed her.

Trent's eyebrows lowered as worry flashed across his face. "We'll have to stay put until Josiah is born. This spot is more secure for now. You should try getting some rest." He lay back down.

She stared at him and wondered what would have

happened to her if he hadn't been camping last night. He was a good man. Tomorrow, she'd tell him so. Her eyes closed and she drifted into a restless sleep.

A thud jerked her awake. Clumps of dirt from the overhanging tree roots dropped through the ripped roof and onto the floor. She sat up and scooted toward the door. A light haze shone through the forest. Trent kneeled by the river, splashing water over his head. She pushed to her feet and joined him.

Rex lapped up a drink and trotted around sniffing.

The cold water chilled her but felt good to her skin. "Can we drink this? Looks so refreshing and clear."

"It's not recommended, although canines and other animals often drink from them."

She pushed back, wiping her hands on her jeans. "They don't get sick?"

"No. He gets his yearly shots that protect him. In your condition, we have to boil the water first." He held snacks out. "There's one more package of peanut butter and crackers, an apple, three packs of trail mix, and a couple of pieces of beef jerky. Which would you like?"

Nick would have tossed her whichever he didn't want, but Trent gave her a choice. Odd how she'd grown used to Nick's uncaring ways. How refreshing to experience someone more thoughtful.

"I'll take the peanut butter crackers and only eat half of them. We can save the rest for later." What she craved was hot buttered biscuits with honey poured over them and a caramel latte. Her mouth watered at the thought, and her stomach growled.

"I'm not arguing with a pregnant woman's growling stomach." He chuckled.

"First thing I'm going to do when we get out of here is eat a hot meal." She looked down at her dirty clothes. "Well, maybe the second. First, after they check me out at the hospital, is a shower, and clean clothes. Thanks again for letting me wear your coat and shirt. It's saved me from all those mosquitoes. I'd like to use your bug spray again if that's okay."

"Sure. I'll get it." He stood and wiped his wet hands on his jeans, then dug into his pack.

She admired his tall stature. The growing scruffy beard and disheveled hair gave him a rugged, but handsome appearance. She scolded herself for admiring him when her husband died a little over twenty-four hours ago.

Truth being, her love for Nick fizzled with his first affair, even more with his second. His addictions caused a lot of arguments and tension in their lives and stress to their marriage. His death wasn't the out she'd wanted.

Long hours at the bakery had her thinking she was part of the problem until she wised up and filed for divorce.

She munched on the third cracker. She dusted the salty crumbs from her fingers. "I probably shouldn't have eaten these salty crackers with my ankles swelling, but it's not like I had a choice."

"Beef jerky is loaded with salt. You selected wisely, wise one." He grinned and drew closer with the mosquito spray.

She laughed at his attempt at humor, took the coat off and handed it back. "I don't need this now." She held her arms out. The smell of bug spray filled her nostrils. She coughed. Her belly tightened and her low back ached. She glanced at Trent as he put the jacket inside the bag and dropped the spray inside. He placed more wood on the fire. She bit her lip and bent double.

"Your pains are much closer now."

She nodded. "So much pressure."

"Let's change the subject. Have you given thought to why the bear attacked that man years ago?"

She huffed several breaths and tried relaxing, but it hadn't worked. "All I've ever focused on was the attack. I hadn't thought about the why. But after being out here and seeing that mama bear with her cubs, I can relate to her protective nature."

"So, the sow felt her baby was being threatened, and she protected it. As you said earlier, you're protecting your baby. It's all a matter of respect for humans and wildlife. Don't mess with a mama and her babies."

"You're right. It gives me a new perspective on nature, but doesn't erase the horror of that scene." She took in a breath and let it out slowly. "I think feeling guilty for the man's injuries gave me a distaste for the mountains and affected my life on so many levels." She rubbed her back. "Man, that hurts. Anyway, being out here thirty-eight weeks pregnant was a big mistake, but traipsing through the forest with you has helped me see that there is beauty beyond my trauma. You haven't made fun of my fears. You've walked me through them. Guess I should thank you."

Rex walked over and lay down by Trent. He reached over and rubbed his side. "Being out here is freeing. It relaxes me, well, normally. I could stay for weeks at a time and never grow tired of the beauty. Someday, I'd like to share my life with someone who loves nature so we can camp and hike together. On the other hand, my job is very demanding which could cause problems in a relationship. Even my parents and sister express their concern for my long hours."

Brooke found herself attracted to Trent and wondered what it would be like to have him around all the time. If his job kept him away from home so much, maybe his family was right. Nick had been away a lot too, but Trent didn't compare with Nick. Could she see herself with someone who was away all the time, again?

"Well, I hope you find someone who meets with your criteria." Why had she raised her voice and been so indignant? It wasn't like her, and she'd only known this man a little more than a day.

His eyebrows lowered and his face reddened. She'd either upset him or made him mad, which wasn't her intention. Were the labor pains making her edgy or was it something else…something he'd said about romance?

Trent stared at her. What triggered her sudden sarcasm? Had labor truly set in, causing her to lash out through her pain? His feelings for her had intensified and he couldn't get her off his mind. Had she discounted that they might be an item if he could adjust his hours at work?

"I came out here to get away from everything and to make some decisions about my future. I love being a K-9 handler, but when I agreed to get my EMT license I didn't know that would lead to delivering babies. I knew it was a possibility, but my real job is search and rescue, not deliver and swaddle."

"Oh, so now I'm the problem." She pushed to her feet.

Rex growled.

"Quiet, Rex."

She stood and propped her hands on her hips, glaring at him. "Is that it? I intruded into your camp and destroyed your getaway. Now I'm your problem."

His jaw tightened. "Yes, and no. It's my job to serve, rescue and protect, but I don't *want* to deliver your baby." Heat rushed to his face. "I've delivered two babies in emergency situations and the last one died in my arms. I'm the guy who always saves the day and makes everyone happy, but holding that lifeless infant and knowing there was nothing I could do took a chunk out of my heart. I have nightmares about it. I never wanted to do it again. Can't you understand?"

As soon as the words regurgitated from his mouth, he regretted them. His gut churned. He'd just lost her trust, assuming he had it, and destroyed a friendship. She hadn't deserved the wrath of his uncoiling doubts and lack of faith.

She gulped air, and her jaw dropped. Her eyes reddened and filled with tears, soaking her cheeks. There, he'd done it. Spilled his guts, made himself look like a fool and made her cry.

"I can't believe the extent to which you've withheld your feelings and resentment toward me and my baby. I thought you were the answer to my cries for help." Her voice quivered. "The death of that preemie was out of your hands. You had no control over it. I'm practically full-term. There's no comparison."

Rex barked and stepped forward. Trent put his hand down. "Quiet." Rex stood tall with his ears up, looking back and forth between them.

"I don't resent you. I'm here and I'm going to deliver Josiah. But I'd prayed the infant would be spared. Now I have to live, knowing I destroyed the joy in that family.

She covered her mouth and sobs erupted before she made her way back inside the tent.

He spun on his good foot, and walked away, far enough he couldn't hear her crying. He fumed and re-greted shouting at her. Guilt and self-doubt ate at him. He'd prided himself in remaining brave and strong, and yet he'd just catapulted her positive view of him into oblivion.

Being with her this short time, seeing her beauty, and knowing he'd become attracted to her regardless of her opinion of nature and their situation, had given him hope for the future. She'd just admitted to a differ-ent outlook because he hadn't judged her. He'd ruined everything. Josiah was her first baby. His fear of fail-ure and the possibility of destroying her life was more than he could handle.

"What have I done?" he whispered.

He took a deep breath and edged closer to the tent. Rex followed close behind him, and nudged at his hand. Trent stalled when he heard her crying and whispering a prayer. She asked for mercy and asked for healing for him from his turmoil and suffering. She cried. "I can't deliver Josiah by myself."

He huffed, spun, scraped fingers through his hair and

rubbed his face. Her whispers met with his ears. "I've grown to care about him, even in the short stress-filled time we've been together. Please help me and help Trent find peace and confidence."

More guilt heaped on him for eavesdropping. She cared about him. He cared about her. Could he ever right the wrong he'd created? He paced outside the tent, then dropped to his knees and blinked tears away. Rex pushed against him and licked his face. He grabbed Rex and hugged him, burying his face in his fur.

"God, what have I done? Turned my back on You, for one. Now, I've hurt Brooke. Failure over the loss of that preemie has consumed me. I don't want to carry this burden anymore. I need help—please help me."

Rex whined, wagged his tail and licked Trent's face again. Trent rubbed his dog's back and ruffled his ears. "I know. Love you, too. I'm okay." He stood, wiped his face and looked to the sky. "Forgive me for thinking I had it all under control and could handle anything. I see now that I am not in control. You are. I've been unreasonable and selfish. Help me be a better person and help me deliver Brooke's baby."

Somehow, he felt lighter. More settled.

Brooke let out a wailing moan. His breath hitched. The roar of the waterfall muted the intensity of her cry somewhat, and for that, he was thankful. Maybe their pursuers were too far away to make out their location. Glad he'd boiled the spring water early enough for it to have time to cool.

He scraped bark from a stick, rinsed it with his energy drink and grabbed his cell from his backpack. He eased inside the tent and found her lying on the ground with her knees up. Hurt, both emotional and physical, conveyed in her eyes. Her red nose and cheeks evidence of her tears and disappointment in him. She bit her lip and looked away.

He kneeled beside her and took her hand in his, cleared his throat and spoke as genuinely as he knew how. "For the record, I have a big mouth and you didn't deserve my outburst. That's not the real me. God just brought me to my knees, and I've given it all to Him. Doesn't mean I'm anywhere near perfect. Got a lot of changes to make in my attitude." He sniffed and blew out a short huff.

"You know I can't do this by myself." She tugged her hand from his, covered her eyes and cried.

Trent placed his hand on her arm. "You and Josiah burst into my camp and have affected me in a way I never thought possible. Haven't met the little guy yet, but if he's anything like you, he's strong, determined and passionate. Can't wait to meet him. I'm honored to help bring him into the world. You asked about my fear, well, this is it, but I'm willing to face it head-on with your help. You should never be expected to give birth alone. I'm here and I'm nervous, but I want to help."

She uncovered her face and cut her eyes at him. Doubt and fear emitted. Her eyebrows lowered. She held her abdomen with one hand, squeezed his hand with a death grip and groaned. "I think it's time."

The drumroll in his chest picked up speed. He grabbed the cloth from the tent's doorway and slid it under her. "Got my cell. May not have reception, but at least we can take a few pictures."

She nodded. Her sad eyes tore at his heart. He couldn't tell if she hadn't forgiven him or if it was labor pains.

He placed the phone on the ground beside her and made sure the warm water was within reach. Rex lay in the doorway watching. Trent glanced at the supplies they'd lined up earlier.

"Blanket. Check. Shoelace cut in half. Check. Knife. Check. Sterile water. Check." He snapped a picture of the make-do delivery table, then opened the first aid kit.

"I'm going to need both hands." She released her grip, and he ripped open an alcohol packet.

He wiped his hands clean with the alcohol pad and prepared himself for delivery.

"I'm scared." Tears rolled onto the edges of her hair.

"No need. You're doing great." He blew out a shaky breath. "Here. Bite on this stick. Maybe it will help. Next time, push as hard as you can." *Here we go.*

Her big blue eyes, red from crying, stayed focused on him. The longer she stared, the more his heart swelled. How could he fall for someone he'd just met? She admitted he'd helped her overcome her fear of the mountains, now she forced him to face his. Could she sense they were a team thrust together in an unbelievable situation? Could she possibly see herself with him?

Her eyebrows lowered and pain emitted from her face. Contraction after contraction, cries and an occasional scream. Morning faded and afternoon took its place. Perspiration beaded on her forehead, and his. The cool mist from the waterfall devoured the midday heat, making the warm temperature inside the tent tolerable.

"One more time." He gritted his teeth. *Let this be it.*

"Ohhhh…" Her teeth bit into the stick.

Josiah fell into his hands. Tiny, perfect infant with blond waves of hair pressed against his head. Shock and elation soared.

She sighed, grabbed the phone and snapped a picture, then dropped it on the floor.

Trent held his breath and lightly squeezed both sides of the newborn's nose and eased away the mucus. *Cry. I need you to cry.* He turned the tiny figure over and held him with one hand while he stroked small circles on Josiah's tender back with the other hand, stimulating his skin.

A squeaky cry filled the tent and tiny fingers clutched his finger. Trent's heart exploded. He choked back tears of joy and relief.

He checked the time. "Josiah Chandler, born at 2:42 p.m., on Sunday, August eighth. How's that for the record book?"

Rex hopped to his feet, stretched his neck, and sniffed the crying baby's feet. One foot hit his nose when Josiah kicked. He sat back and cocked his head, watching them.

Trent fought the overwhelming emotion surging through his veins. He looked down at Brooke. Her weary face beamed as she held out her arms. He handed the newborn to her and tied off the umbilical cord.

He snapped pictures as best he could. Knowing the way his sister obsessed over pictures of Mandy's every move, he followed suit for Brooke.

She glowed and stole what seemed like a million kisses before she handed him back. Trent passed the phone to her while he washed the newborn down with the sterile water to reduce the risk of bacterial infection. Then wrapped him snugly in the blue blanket, and handed him back. She kissed and caressed her son while he snapped a few more pictures.

"We did it." She reached for Trent and he took her hand. "We did it, and you were an amazing coach."

Josiah curled his fingers into fists and spread them wide again. He squeaked and looked like a toy curled up in the blanket. He snuggled against Brooke's neck and closed his eyes.

Trent kissed her hand. "You are a beautiful mother, and you did better than I ever imagined. Josiah is…is perfect. I'm happy for you." He leaned down and kissed her forehead. "Congratulations. As my sister would say, 'Time for a selfie.' Come on, Rex."

Rex eased over and laid his head on Brooke's arm. His big, dark eyes stared at the bundle, then up at her and over to Trent.

He held the phone in the air. "Smile." After several snaps, he tucked the phone in his back pocket.

Brooke placed her hand on Rex's furry head. "What do you think of our new hiking buddy?"

Rex whined, sniffed and wiggled closer.

Trent dropped his shoulders and breathed a sigh of relief. God answered his prayer. Mother and baby were doing well, and his fear had faded, for now.

"I don't want to intrude on the moment, but we need to finish getting you cleaned up so you can relax and admire your son."

Chapter Nine

Brooke used the rest of the sterilized water and washed off as best as she could while Trent disposed of the birthing cloth that had been under her. Good thinking on his part. She rested on the uncomfortably hard ground, holding her son. She gazed at his delicate face, mesmerized by him. It had happened. She did it. She'd faced her worst fears, giving birth in the wilderness and overcoming her apprehension of the mountains.

Life looked brighter for the moment, and her confidence kicked up a notch. She'd given birth to a healthy son, and Trent helped her through it all. He was amazing and encouraged her for hours. She'd made the right decision to trust him. And he'd thought to take pictures. What a miracle to behold.

She held Josiah's tiny hand. His fingers closed around her finger. How could she feel such love? Her heart squeezed. He squirmed in her arms and let out a high-pitched cry.

Trent stuck his head inside the doorway. Rex followed suit. "Everything okay in there?"

"Yes. I'm going to try feeding him."

He backed away. "Come on, Rex. Let's leave them alone."

Rex spun and followed his handler.

While Josiah ate, Brooke thought about her parents and how disappointed they'd be to learn she'd had him and they weren't part of his grand arrival. She chewed on her lip. Nick could have been a part of Josiah's life. They could have shared the joy and happiness together if he'd only made better choices. Josiah favored him a little.

So much had happened over the last forty-eight hours. Arguing with Nick, insisting he sign the divorce papers and how frustrated she'd been with him and his excuses. The fear in his voice when he told her to run. Her disappearing in the forest with no sense of direction. Her wobbly legs and doubts of survival. Then there was Trent.

She lifted Josiah to her shoulder and patted his back. A puff of air with a faint burp sounded. She lowered him back into her arms and gazed at her little miracle.

"Knock, knock," Trent said. "Am I clear to come inside?"

"Of course."

He stepped into the tent with Rex swooshing by his leg. Rex sniffed Josiah's head and licked him. Brooke looked into his dark eyes. "What do you think, Rex? Do you approve?"

Rex wagged his tail and backstepped like he knew how to dance. He whined and let out a low bark. Trent grabbed him and ruffled his fur.

Trent's unshaven beard and unkempt hair encircled his green eyes.

"Want to hold him?"

His face brightened.

"Sure you don't mind?" He took Josiah in his arms and cradled him.

Trent's smile said it all. Had he jumped the hurdle that held him hostage? She bit her lip and studied him as her baby clutched his finger. Trent's gaze at him emitted tenderness. Her heart squeezed.

"Let me take a picture of you holding him."

He handed her his phone, and she snapped a picture.

"What's our next move?" She shuffled and placed her arm behind her head. "Do we stay here until help comes, or do we continue climbing this mountain?"

His smile disappeared. The corners of his mouth turned down, and his expression became serious. He looked at Josiah, then back at her. "I can't be sure the two men we ran into will tell the rangers we're here. If we stay here, off the trail and out of sight from hikers, there's no telling how long it will be before help arrives. We could be here for days or even weeks."

Her stomach plummeted. He was right. But how could she go on with limited strength, carrying Josiah?

"The thought of leaving the security of this dilapidated shelter makes me nervous. I know we can't stay here, but I don't know how well I'll hold up. When do we need to go?" Her lip quivered at the thought of continuing the journey.

"Not today. You need time to regain some strength. One night isn't long enough for recovery, but every step forward gets us closer to rescue. It also puts us at risk of encountering other obstacles or meeting up with the killers."

She blew out a shaky breath. "Tomorrow it is. I can't guarantee how far I can go, but I'll try."

He handed Josiah back to her. "We'll do what you can, but for now, you need to eat. How about the last apple and another trail mix?"

"Sounds good." He started out of the tent, and she grabbed his hand. "Thank you again for taking care of us. You could've already been home by now."

"Wouldn't have it any other way." He disappeared outside the tent with Rex on his heels.

She took in a deep breath and released it slowly. "I can do this. I can finish this journey," she whispered. "Lord, Your Word says I can do all things through You, and You'll give me strength. I need all the strength I can get. Thank You for answering my prayer, and thank You for my healthy baby."

Trent leaned inside and handed her the snacks along with a bottled water. "Drink all the water. You need it. I'll boil water from the waterfall in the coffee pot and refill our empty bottles."

"You can do that? Is it safe?"

"Yep. Boil three minutes and let it cool. May take the rest of the afternoon to get them refilled, but I'll get it done." He slipped back out.

Brooke munched on the apple and trail mix. Could she ever eat them again without the reminder of this day? She splashed a little of the water from her bottle on her face and sipped on the rest. She longed for a shower and her pillow top mattress.

Weariness washed over her. She lay on her side with Josiah snug against her chest and closed her eyes.

Water splashing woke her. She raised up and peered outside the tent. What was Trent doing standing in the river? He held a long stick and threw it into the water. Pulled it out and waited, then threw it in again. When he lifted it up again, a fish was on the other end. He'd speared a fish.

Admiration for his survival skills amazed her. Enjoying a fish dinner made her mouth water. The protein would help give her extra strength needed to begin the next trek through the woods.

She forced herself to her feet and emerged from the tent, holding Josiah. Trent stepped out of the water and walked toward her, holding his catch in the air, smiling.

"Thought I'd try my hand at spear fishing." He laughed. "Had to improvise since I abandoned all my gear back at the camp. It worked. We have two trout. Who knew? Tonight, we're having a feast."

"You actually speared a fish. I can hardly wait to sink my teeth into something besides crackers and trail mix." She kissed Josiah's head.

"Gotta clean them. The propane tank is running low on fuel. I'm going to cook these on our small fire."

"What do you need me to do?" How could she help with her body feeling drained?

"Nothing. Maybe walk around and work up some strength for tomorrow's hike." He popped out his knife and tossed the fish on a rock. "Relax and enjoy Josiah. I've got this."

His cell phone was lying on top of his backpack. He'd changed the cover photo to the selfie he took of the four of them. Josiah, Rex, himself and her. She couldn't help but smile. So much stress had dissolved today, and her fear of childbirth no longer terrified her.

She strolled to the water's edge and walked closer to the waterfall. A fine mist moistened her face. She covered Josiah's head with the blanket and enjoyed the beauty of her surroundings.

"Mom, I'll be home soon, and you can meet your grandson," she whispered. "No one will ever believe my story. I'm uncertain how the birth certificate will read. Smoky Mountain waterfall baby? Born in the wild?"

Would she ever return here? Maybe. Depending on whether search and rescue located them before the killers. Her pulse increased. She couldn't think about that. No one would ever take her baby away from her.

She searched the tree line above. Amazingly, she hadn't broken a bone or hurt Josiah when she fell. Were those men up there watching? No gunshots, so evidently, they didn't know where to look.

Her little bundle squirmed. She patted his back and swayed, cuddling him close to her chest. So dainty and fragile. Her responsibilities now changed forever. Caring and nurturing took on a whole new meaning. Getting him home to his newly decorated room added another hurdle to her agenda.

The smell of smoke tickled her nose. She spun. Trent sat by the fire, cooking the fish. She sauntered her way back to the camp and inspected the open-air roasting. Two forked sticks stuck in the ground on each side of the flames. The two long sticks, holding both fish, rested on the forked ones. His resourceful abilities impressed her again.

"You never cease to amaze me."

"Oh, nothing to it." He poked the fire. "Camping survival books explain how to do everything, well, except deliver babies in the wild. Our dinner is almost ready."

"I'm glad you did your homework. And I'm glad you trusted God to help you through your situation. He helped me see that anything is possible with Him. I was caught up in feelings of rejection and betrayal and had determined I couldn't trust myself to make important decisions."

He stilled and looked at her. "Glad you've found breakthrough. Seems He knocked down a few bricks in my thinking, too. The sergeant will be glad I'm showing signs of improvement. I'm certain he's lining up a lot of overtime for me. He knows I love my job and I'd work twenty-four hours a day if needed."

She broke eye contact. Needn't pursue her admiration of him. His love was his job with no room for her. She longed for someone to share her and her son's life with, not a workaholic.

Her tastebuds came to life with the first bite. She'd never been so hungry for actual food, and the natural flavor tasted like a delicacy. No salt, no spices. Meat only. Trent shared some of his fish with Rex, then gave him another packet of dog food and a snack. He made camping look fun, but then, he hadn't trudged up a mountain thirty-eight weeks pregnant and had a baby. Maybe, minus those hurdles, the adventure wouldn't be as dreadful.

"Can't believe I ate the whole thing, well, except for the bones." She licked her fingers. "Delicious."

"We needed something solid. Hiking takes a lot out

of you." He took the bones to the edge of the cliff wall and buried them. "Easy cleanup. I suggest you get as much rest as you can tonight. We have a long day tomorrow."

"Do you think anyone's reported us missing yet?" Her thoughts swirled. "My parents are probably beside themselves with worry."

"Since I haven't reported in, my parents know something's not right. I'm confident they've already called the ranger's station." He reached over and squeezed her hand. "We are going to make it. I expect sometime tomorrow help will arrive."

"You really think so?" His assurance encouraged her. Anticipation mounted. She looked to the sky. "Thank You for watching over us, Lord. Send help soon."

Daylight dwindled and darkness fell over the camp. Josiah wiggled and squirmed. His squeaky cry grew louder.

"Guess I'd better feed him and turn in for the night. Thank you for the fish. Maybe all of us will get some rest." She walked over to the opening of the tent and paused. She turned and faced him. "Thank you, Trent, for everything. I couldn't have made it without you. You're a godsend and I really appreciate your honesty and courage."

Trent pushed to his feet and walked toward her. His gaze bored into hers. He pulled her close. "I should be thanking you. My life has taken on a new meaning since I met you. I'm not wallowing in my failures and dreading Josiah's delivery."

He looked down at her with the tiny bundle and

couldn't help himself. His hands cupped her cheeks as he leaned in and kissed her soft lips.

She placed her hand against his chest, pushed back and stared at him with a questioning look. Her lips parted, but he placed his finger over them.

"Congratulations. You amaze me. You and Josiah get some rest." Could she feel the hard beats thudding against his chest? She'd captured his heart without trying. He turned back toward the campfire. Her warm hand gripped his arm.

"I know you're a K-9 handler in search and rescue and birthing babies isn't in your job description, but you managed today like a pro, with intelligence and compassion and for the record, his full name is Josiah Trent Chandler. I'm naming him after the one who rescued us in this wilderness and brought him into the world. We will never forget you."

He fought tears. It wasn't like him to get emotional. Not like this. He never expected her to name Josiah after him. His eyes, once again, bored into her gentle, caring gaze. "Don't know what to say, except I'm honored."

"And I'm forever grateful."

He kissed her again on the lips and turned back to the campfire before his emotions got the best of him. Rex curled up beside him on the ground. He ran fingers through the soft fur and stared into the blaze. He'd heard of love at first sight, but he never saw himself in this situation. It wasn't at first sight for him, but he *had* found her attractive, just hadn't expected to develop feelings overnight.

Had he been so overjoyed by a safe delivery and healthy baby that he'd lost his senses and thought he had feelings for her? He gave Rex a treat. Brooke. He couldn't get her off his mind, and yet, she'd just commented she'd never forget him like being rescued would end their relationship. Her soft lips molded perfectly against his. Had he been presumptuous?

He'd made himself available at work for extended hours since he lived alone and had nothing better to do. Attraction to Brooke had him rethinking his hours and his future with a ready-made family. She'd participated in both kisses, so it wasn't one-sided. Was it? Mixed emotions ate at him.

He slid down closer to the fire and stared at the sky until his eyes grew heavy. Getting them out of these mountains without encountering more danger was a priority. However, Zeke and the two other nameless men, he assumed, were still on the hunt. He and Brooke had chanced a fire two nights in a row. Would they spot the campfire and stray from the main trail in search of them? Would Josiah's cry draw them closer? His gut twisted.

Lord, could You keep those guys away and send help tomorrow?

Early dawn came too soon. An idea popped into Trent's head. He dug into the backpack and pulled out his one extra pair of jeans and extra shirt. Opened the first aid kit and snagged the small scissors. He could hardly wait to see the surprise on her face when she saw what he'd made.

Rex bounced around, racing up and down the riverbank. Trent picked up a stick and tossed it. "Fetch." He chased after it and brought it back. "Good boy. Have a treat. These are your favorites."

Rex barked.

"Shhh, quiet. You'll wake her."

He glanced inside the open space of the tent. Brooke sat quietly, looking down at her baby. Her baby. She was a mother now. Her hand smoothed over his blond hair, circled her finger around his small ears, and she kissed those soft cheeks.

How could he invade her private moment? So serene. So momentous. Had he ever taken the time to capture such delicate moments? The love she displayed captivated him. He looked away. Rex nudged his hand.

"These will make her happy, Rex. We'll be back home before you know it."

Brooke emerged from the tent with her bundle, no bigger than a football, wrapped up in Mandy's doll blanket. "Good morning."

"You're awake. Hope you got some rest."

"I slept well, except for feeding times." She stepped closer and looked at the strips of cloth lying across his backpack. "What are these?"

"May not be perfect, but I made some diapers out of the only clean shirt I had left, and I made one of those sling things from my last pair of jeans. My sister had one with Mandy, so I figured it would come in handy today."

He held up small, square pieces of fabric with ripped corners. "Tie them on with these."

Her jaw dropped. "You're going to make me cry. How thoughtful and clever. I am blown away."

His chest swelled. He had impressed her.

"Thank you so much. I didn't know what I was going to do!" She laughed.

"And look." He held up the length of his denim jeans with the legs cut open. The ends were slit like the diapers. The sling was a little smaller than normal ones but should work.

"I love it. Your ingenuity amazes me. Tie it around me and let's see how it works." She held Josiah up against her chest.

He stood in front of her and put the center of the fabric under Josiah's body, then looped it up around her neck and tied it. The second leg went around her abdomen and he fastened it in the back.

"How does that feel?" He stepped away and lifted his eyebrows.

She walked around and bounced a little. "Feels fantastic. Tighten it a little more and it will be perfect. I think you've just invented the emergency baby wrap."

She threw her arms around his neck and hugged him. "Thank you."

The warmth of her embrace messed with his emotions. She tried stepping back, but he didn't want this moment to end. He held her a little longer. Was he getting too involved? Were his feelings mounting because she'd forced him to face his fears?

"I'm happy if you are." He kissed her forehead and turned away. "Take a few minutes to stretch your legs before we head out."

"After I put one of your special handmade diapers on Josiah. Untie me please."

He untied the wrap and laid it on his backpack. She opened the blanket and exposed the infant's naked body. Tiny hands grasped at the air. She slid the small diaper underneath, folded it around the front, and tied the sides. The fabric swallowed his little body but would work until they were back in civilization.

"Perfect. Now you've invented emergency diapers in the wild."

He'd given her some momentary joy before facing a rough day.

She swaddled Josiah, stood and straightened her back.

"Are you ready for another trek through the woods?"

She inhaled and blew out a long breath. "My sore body says it hurts to move. The scrapes on my hands and back sting and ache." She pulled up her shirt sleeves, exposing bruises across her arms. "Not sure which hurt more. The fall or giving birth. I'm as ready as I can be." She turned and faced the waterfall. "I've gotten used to the roar."

Trent analyzed her while she had her back to him. Was he wrong to move her so soon after giving birth? His EMT instructor said women should get up and walk around right after delivery. It could help the healing process go faster and decrease the risk of blood clots. However, he didn't say she should go mountain climbing and starve. At least she had fish for dinner last night.

He'd watch her body language and take it slow. Her ponytail tossed with the breeze. She'd been through a horrific ordeal, and yet she still held up under pressure. He admired her mostly positive attitude and courage.

Rex trotted along the river's edge, stopping occasionally for a drink. His ears perked up, and he held his tail and head high, then proceeded to sniff the ground.

Trent poured the last of the cooled boiled water from the coffeepot into another empty bottle. They had four full bottles of water. He blew out a breath. That should get them through the day. Brooke sat on a boulder, holding Josiah and watching Rex roam. He grabbed his cell and snapped a picture of the picturesque moment. She was stunning. He bit his lip and studied her. Was he ready for an instant family?

She turned back and caught him staring. "You look deep in thought. Anything you want to share?"

He definitely wasn't ready to share the question that came into his mind. "Thinking about the route we should take."

"Do we have a choice?"

He rubbed his forehead. "Since we dropped several feet from the trail, the shortest route is still over the mountain, but it's also the hardest. Altitude could be a problem. Rather than climbing back up to Redbud Trail, I think the easier route, terrain wise, is around the mountain. But it's also longer and more susceptible to wild hog encounters. We'd be a distance from the main trail, which could make it harder for search and rescue."

She took in a breath, and opened her mouth, but clamped it shut. Josiah whimpered. She patted his back and swayed with him.

"Are you asking me to choose?" She moved closer.

"Not necessarily. But time is of the essence." He drew in the sand with a stick. "If we go this way, through the forest, we'd be making our own path until we run into another trail. If we go this way, straight up, the cell tower will be accessible sooner, but you could experience altitude sickness and we could run into your pursuers."

She closed her eyes and rubbed her forehead. "Wild hogs or killers with guns." She dropped her hand from her face. "Cell tower or the probability of another night in the woods. Risk altitude sickness or traipse through unexplored territory." Her eyes bored into his. "Would Josiah have problems breathing in the high altitude? I've already experienced headaches."

"When you put it like that, we don't have a choice. No need to create any more problems than what we already have." He tossed the stick aside. "Around, it is, but we'll still be climbing."

He stood and popped his neck. He wasn't about to risk the high altitude with a newborn. Going around could help, but not totally avoid high terrain. His ankle ached, but not as bad as earlier. A hot shower crossed his mind. His scruffy beard itched.

He picked up the remaining firewood. "Gonna toss these back in the woods and clean up the area." He walked along the river's edge until he'd rounded the curve and tossed the limbs on the ground. The trail up on the ridge was hidden by all the trees.

Rex ran and met him when he returned. Tail wagging and tongue hanging out. Brooke sat on a log near the bank, holding Josiah.

"Did you miss me?" Rex trotted beside him, constantly looking up at him. "Yeah, you did. I can tell. We'll be leaving this scenic place in a few minutes. You can help me protect our guests today."

Rex talked back with a howl and a bark.

He grabbed the coffeepot, scooped water from the river and poured it over the fire, then kicked dirt on top.

No chance of catching the forest on fire, even though only dirt and rocks surrounded them.

"You holding up, okay?"

"Better than I expected. It's eerie out here by myself."

"You get used to it after a while." He sat and dug into the backpack for their morning snacks.

"I suppose, under the right conditions." Skeptical, but she didn't argue.

She sat on a rock across from him. He couldn't help admiring the loose strands of brown hair framing her face and remembering how the reflection of last night's fire danced in her eyes. He scraped a hand over his beard. Normally, he didn't care what he looked like while out camping, but things were different this time. He regretted not having his razor.

"I'll finish the peanut butter crackers from yesterday."

He dug them from the backpack. "Here's your left-over water. We've got more now if you need it. Guess I'll finish the beef jerky I pocketed."

"This is good enough for me." She grew solemn. "Honestly, I'm dreading the journey today."

A howl roared through the camp. She stiffened. "That sounded close. Was it a coyote? Do they run in packs?"

"Coyotes live in family groups, but word has it they usually travel and hunt alone. Attacks on humans are rare. No need to worry."

"So you say."

Chapter Ten

Brooke held Josiah close as she prepared for the hike. Her newfound protective nature kept him warm and shielded him from the fine mist drifting from the waterfall. His every move had her on high alert, and his little squeaks and cries took on new meanings. Hungry. Wet. Stretching. Snuggling. Who knew she'd become so attuned to his needs so quickly?

Light filtered through the trees. A coyote had made its presence known, and she faced another long day. The start of her third day in the wilderness much later than when she'd told her mom she'd be back home. She ached for the mental torture her parents suffered over her disappearance.

She'd made the trip alone. A mistake she'd never live down. Or was it? Would the men have killed whoever joined her? If they'd shoot Nick in cold blood and shoot at Trent, they'd certainly wipe out anyone in the house, except her, until Josiah was born. A chill raced over her body.

Rex reclined at Trent's feet while he finished eating his beef jerky. He was a remarkable man, like none she'd ever met. Could she fall in love so soon after her ex-husband's death? Were her feelings justifiable, or was she merely vulnerable to this brave and compassionate K-9 handler who saved her, delivered Josiah and put his life at risk for them? Her sentiments for him felt right, but she wouldn't know for sure until she was back home in her natural environment. He'd only kissed her. He hadn't said anything about continuing a relationship after they were rescued. He'd only commented about working twenty-four-seven. Not the life she wanted.

She pushed to her feet, holding Josiah. Her legs wobbled and her body rebelled, but she had to move around. Maybe walking today would do her good, although lying back down sounded better.

Rex stood and wagged his tail. A whine escaped. She caught Trent's gaze as Rex allowed her to pat his head. He sniffed her legs. Trent worked with another piece of fabric. "What clever creations are you making now?"

He held up a flat piece of fabric with two slits cut about four inches apart. It's a shirt for Josiah. What do you think?"

Rex walked beside her with his nose in the air, sniffing her baby.

"Rex. Sit." His dog obeyed and sat by his side with his back straight and ears up.

"Perfect design for an infant born in the mountains. I'm impressed."

"Seemed logical your little man needed something around his chest besides the blanket." He handed the creation to her and petted Rex.

She sat on the log and unwrapped her living doll.

His little hands grasped at the air as she slid his arms through the openings and overlapped the extra fabric across his chest. "Fits perfectly."

She lifted Josiah and Trent snapped a photo of him dressed in his matching diaper and shirt. It wasn't the soft onesie from home but would do for now. She quickly swaddled him in the blanket and held him close.

"I could use another drink of water." Had dehydration caught up with her? Weakness coiled itself around her. She guzzled more water than she'd intended, but her body longed for the extra fluid. She capped the bottle and handed it back to Trent.

He pushed it back at her and handed her a small package of trail mix. "Drink all you want. Your body needs it after all you've been through."

She took the trail mix but refused the water, knowing he'd do without to make sure she had what she needed. Wasn't right for him to give up so much when she was the one who'd caused all his problems and put him in this position.

"I'm good for now." Her taste buds tingled at the thought of a latte and a hot cinnamon roll. "What's next?"

"The sooner we get moving, the better." Trent stood and dropped his phone in the outside pocket of his backpack. "If help hasn't arrived by this afternoon, I'll build us a suitable shelter."

"I'm counting on being in my bed tonight. How can I help pack up?"

"Put the propane, cup, Rex's water bowl and whatever else you see in the backpack. I'm going to dispose of this tent."

Rex hopped up and ran to the river, lapping the cold water. He sniffed the ground, the air, and drank more before traipsing off to explore. He returned and followed Trent around.

"Would you put the baby wrap around me, so I don't have to lay him on the ground?"

Trent's face lit up. He retrieved the wrap and tied it snug around her body and neck. Josiah rested against her chest and slept. She gathered all the supplies and arranged them in the bag, noting how low they were on food. At least they had fish last night and still had four bottles of water.

Trent tossed the supporting limbs from their make-do shelter.

"Are we taking it with us?"

"Part of it." He pulled out his pocketknife and cut one whole sidewall out of the rough fabric, folded the thickness, and stuffed it into his bulging backpack. He folded his knife and dropped it into his pocket before crumpling the remaining piece in a pile and placing it under the overhang of the tree root where it once stood.

"This will have to do until I can return and discard it properly." He dusted his hands and turned to her. "I know I keep asking this, but are you ready?"

His light green eyes blended with the various shades of green in the forest. He'd proven himself as a man of integrity and he'd won her trust, mostly. She'd called him trustworthy, but she'd know for sure if he got them to safety. How many times had Nick made promises and never followed through? She'd lost count. Her insides churned at the thought of making another wrong decision, like she had with Nick. It felt right trusting Trent, but was she falling into another failed relationship?

She propped her hands at her waist. "What woman who just birthed a baby do you think would be up for this task?" She lifted her eyebrows and waited for an answer.

He rubbed his unshaven chin. "Guess you've got a point." He checked his compass, hooked the leash on Rex and handed her a walking stick. "Made us new ones."

She placed one hand under Josiah's body and gripped the stick. "You're so resourceful." She followed behind him and hobbled over the rocky surface. "Too bad we have to leave the beauty and sound of the waterfall."

"Oh, so you decided it's beautiful. We can come back after all this is over. Uh, I mean, it's always here if you ever want to return."

"I've seen too much already." She grinned at his slipup. At least he didn't act like he resented the trouble she'd caused him.

He stopped and looked around. "No signs of those guys so far. Keep your ears open. They will have reached the top by now. I'm certain they'll head back down to where they lost sight of us. They know we're moving slow and will widen their search."

"There you go again. Casting more fear into my already skeptical thoughts." She huffed. "You're such a guy. I don't need to know the scary parts. All I need is encouraging, positive comments to keep me going." A shot of espresso would boost her energy. Wasn't her favorite beverage, but it might help regain her waning strength, and they'd only just begun the hike. She had no choice but to push forward as much as her body allowed, and then some.

Trent paused at the curve in the river. His chest swelled when he took in a deep breath. Rex stood beside him and seemed to mimic his handler. The man and his canine knew each other well. She'd grown to appreciate their trust in each other.

"Looks like Richard and Dale trekked through this way. It's too far downhill to get back on the main track." He pulled out his compass and glanced back at her. "Need to cross the river and go up the other side."

Her mouth flew open. "Cross the river?" The pounding in her chest increased. No way would she risk falling with her baby.

"It narrows farther down and will be safer." His stare searched her. "We'll cross over and see where it leads us."

"I thought you knew this place." *Breathe, just breathe. He's doing his best.* Uncertainty gripped her gut.

"I've been on several trails in these mountains, but never ventured off Redbud Trail. We're exploring unfamiliar territory."

He led her along the riverbank. He was right. It narrowed into a stream. "I'll go first."

"Don't fall in. Not in my plan today."

Only four steps across the knee-deep, mildly flowing water and he made it to the other side. She followed without any problems, and they discovered a small trail.

Rex's tail stuck out as he sniffed the ground and stared into the wooded terrain. The dog's behavior and the flattened grass convinced her they were following some animal's trail not meant for hiking. Were they headed toward danger? How many extra miles would this path distance them from the ranger's station? Could she even make it that far?

Trent pushed up the steep incline, with Rex leading the way. Doubts of making the right decision ate at him. His stomach churned. If he stayed due north, they should be fine, but this menial path proved tougher than the Redbud. He glanced back at Brooke. Risks went with whichever decision they made. Would they have been better off to take their chances with the killers on the loose? Maybe. Change in the altitude could cause problems.

Her knuckles whitened as she gripped her stick with one hand and patted Josiah with the other. How much longer would she last? He scolded himself for taking them off course. Had he gotten them lost? Were they going the right direction? His compass said go this way. Must be right. Hunger ripped at his gut and the lack of water was getting the best of him. He paused and took a big swallow.

She trudged along behind him, moving in slow motion. If she could muster up the strength to move faster, maybe they'd hit a better trail and find help.

"I know it's hard on you, but the faster we move, the sooner we'll find help."

"Now *that's* encouraging," she said.

Good thing she didn't know there were wild pigs in this area. Not to mention the usual bears, mountain lions, coyotes and all the other wildlife. If she thought about it, she wouldn't let too much distance come between them.

"Do you need my hand?" Of course, she did. Why ask? His stomach growled again.

"No. I can do this myself."

She held the walking stick with both hands, placed it in front of her, and visibly trudged forward. Josiah hung against her body in the wrap he'd made.

Rex walked into the edge of the tall grass with his ears perked at high alert. Trent scanned the forest while waiting for Brooke to catch up. He spotted a blackberry vine. "Hey, I found us some berries."

He traipsed off the path, pulling the empty water bottle from the loop on his belt. He filled it with the globe-shaped berries, blew on a couple and popped them into his mouth. The splash of sweet flavor tickled his taste buds.

Brooke leaned against a boulder. "I'll wait here. Saving my steps."

He popped several more in his mouth before returning to the trail. "Here, eat these. The sugar will help with energy and they're full of vitamin C and antioxidants."

"Are they safe?" She held it up and inspected it.

He dropped his shoulders and stared at her. "I wouldn't give you anything that would hurt you. Just because you're not in a grocery store doesn't mean they aren't good. There are plenty of berries that aren't edible. You just have to study and be able to recognize them. Blow on it to make sure there are no ants or bugs, then eat it."

She threw it down. "I'm not taking a chance of eating bugs."

"I promise you the berries are safe."

A loud, long puff of breath sounded with each berry she blew on. He'd gotten his fill and felt more refreshed. She downed several, kissed Josiah on the head and patted his back.

"Need to refill the bottle for later." He took off through the tall grass with Rex at his heels and stuffed more of the tasty treats into the bottle. A rustle in the woods caught his attention. His heart jumped into his throat. Berries were a bear's dining table. He should have thought about that before they lingered too long. He rushed back to the path. "Come on. Got to get moving. I heard something. We aren't the only ones who love the sweet taste of berries."

"Don't scare me." She grabbed her stick and followed him. "I can't move as fast as you."

"Do the best you can. Come on." He turned and high-stepped upward. He'd grown weary with little to no sleep, and he couldn't decide if his kiss meant anything to her. Relationship or not, she needed to keep up with him. Getting back to his job didn't sound so bad.

An exasperated gasp filled his ears as they trekked up the mountain. After they were a safe distance away, Trent glanced back. A big buck stood on the path below them. Trent's shoulders relaxed and his eyes fell on Brooke. Her head was down, still gripping the stick until she caught up with him. She stopped and looked up at him. Tears rolled down her cheeks.

His breath caught. Her big blue eyes glistened through the wetness, and her red face told him he'd pushed her too hard. He reached out and pulled her close.

"Let's find a place to rest. You're doing great."

Her lip quivered as she wiped her cheeks. "I'm tired and my body aches. I told you I can't move fast. And I need to feed Josiah again. My husband is dead. I can't call anyone, and I've ruined your camping trip. Leaning on you for everything is difficult for me. I don't want to move another inch, but my life and the life of my baby depend on it. Do you call all that doing great?"

He cleared his throat. "I know this is a lot. But try looking at the bright side. You're alive. Josiah is warm and safe. We haven't starved or been attacked by bears, and we've avoided the killers. If I could carry you, I would." He dropped his arm from around her shoulders and helped her sit on a tree stump. "I'll keep watch while you feed Josiah and take a break."

Rex pivoted and stared up in the trees, growling.

"What is it, boy?" The hum of a bullet whizzed past his ear and hit a tree. Too close. He grabbed Brooke and fell behind a rock. Bullets chipped the stone and bounced off. Rex danced on the leash, baring his teeth, barking, and growling. Trent reeled him in. "Quiet. Good eye."

"They found us." Fear spilled through Brooke's voice. Josiah whimpered, and she consoled him as best she could under the circumstances.

"Not sure where they are." He squinted and peered through the trees until he spotted them up on the ridge. "They're at a higher elevation overlooking the valley. My guess is they are still on Redbud Trail, a distance away, but yes, we're on their radar."

Another shot pinged the rock above Trent's head.

"They're shooting at you." Her breathing edged in hyperventilation. "What are we going to do?"

"First, you're going to focus on breathing normally." He kissed her forehead. "It's okay. You'll be fine. They figure if they can get rid of me, you'll be an easy catch. Right now, they're up on the ridge, too far away to rush in after us. Let's stay close to these boulders and crawl until we reach the dense forest. We'll figure out what to do from there."

"Crawl?" She groaned. "You're putting me through a crash survival course and testing my endurance, aren't you?"

"You said it, not me. If only it were a test. It's easier learning without the death threat, though." He touched her back. "Did I hurt you or Josiah when I jerked you down?"

"No. I'm mad at myself for being emotional and crying like a baby. It's not like me to feel sorry for myself, and here you are, the target of their wrath. You seem to hold up just fine under pressure. If anything happens to you, I'll never forgive myself."

"Nothing's going to happen to me, and you *do* have extenuating circumstances that could cause a smorgasbord of emotions." He couldn't imagine going through all the trauma she'd encountered the past two days. She deserved a medal for bravery.

"Still, I'll focus on doing better, and you have to stay alive." She patted Josiah and kissed his head. He squirmed and let out a squeaky cry. "Not now, little guy, not now."

"I'm not going anywhere. If it helps any, I think

you're an extraordinarily brave lady after all you've endured. I admire your determination and the way you've faced your fears of the wild." She'd forced him to face his self-doubts and fears, and for that, he was grateful.

"You're just being nice. I'm still scared stiff."

"Rightfully so." He checked his compass again. "Guess we better keep moving. Follow me."

He kept Rex close to his side as they crawled along the base of the rocks. Spiders raced up the stone, black ants scattered and a few ladybugs crawled across blades of grass. If she spotted them, she might hop to her feet and scream. He'd best keep her focused on the thicket ahead.

"See that group of pine trees? Concentrate on them. We'll be out of the killer's shooting range once we get there."

"My friends will never believe I hiked, had a baby and crawled on all fours in the woods. I don't believe it myself."

The shade of the pine trees confirmed their closeness to safety. Trent hopped up and helped Brooke to her feet. Josiah's whimpers escalated into full-blown cries. His arms escaped the wrap and his hands opened and closed.

"He's hungry and probably wet. Can you untie the wrap and let me change and feed him?" She turned so fast her ponytail slapped him across the face. He brushed the hair away and smiled. She could do that any day.

"While you take care of Josiah, I'm going to scout around and get a take on our position." Rex took advantage of the lengthened leash, sniffing the ground, the base of trees, and marking his territory.

She grabbed his arm. "Don't leave me here by myself."

Chapter Eleven

The idea of being alone even for a minute in the middle of nowhere made Brooke's insides knot up and twist. *I'm not a wimp even though I've argued, cried and whined.* She reasoned that the only real danger she'd faced wasn't the bears she'd feared for so long. It was being captured by those killers.

She gazed down at the miniature human she'd birthed. His little fingers tightened in a fist and pressed against his cheeks as she fed him. His wispy blond hair lay curled against his scalp. She cupped his small, fragile head with her hand and held him close until he finished eating. After a burp and a diaper change, he went back to sleep. If she were home, she'd sit for hours, rocking and admiring him. If only.

Rex ran to her and licked Josiah's head. His tail wagged, and his dark eyes kept a keen watch. He ran back to Trent, who leaned against the opposite side of one of the pine trees nearby.

Her cheeks warmed. "You can come back now. Thanks for respecting my privacy.

"You're welcome. Hold still so I can snap a couple of memorable photos." His green eyes brightened with his smile.

He pushed away from the tree and walked toward her, holding the baby wrap. His long legs, masculine build, and good looks weakened her in ways she hadn't felt in years. His protective nature and survival skills assured her he'd do whatever it took to get them to safety.

"Guess that means you're ready to keep moving." She drew in a deep breath, exhaled and stood so he could tie the wrap. "Did you find anything?"

"After we pass through these pine trees, we'll face another incline."

"I thought we were taking the easy way around." She stared at him.

"There's nothing easy about hiking, whether up or around. Even going around, we still climb upward only at a more tolerable ascent."

"Any sign of those guys?"

"Nope." He rubbed his eyes, then looked at her. "They may have…"

Rex growled and rushed toward the depths of the pines as far as his leash allowed. A grunting, squealing sound met with Trent's ears. He tugged on the leash. "Rex. Come."

Rex returned with his ears laid back, his fur raised on his spine, and tail straight. He continued growling, looked to Trent, then back into the forest.

"What is it? A wild hog?" Fear emanated in her voice.

"Yep. I could shoot it, but the shot would give our

location away. We need to get moving. Those things are destructive and dangerous."

His jaw tightened. He gripped her hand firmly. Adrenaline rushed over her and pushed her weak body forward like a bungee cord. No doubts, she'd collapse once they were out of danger.

Rex danced on the leash, fighting to get to the animal. He looked like he'd rip the creature to shreds if Trent would let him loose.

"Quiet, Rex."

Rex obeyed. He kept the length of the leash tight. If she read him right, he wanted to fight and protect them.

The squealing and snorting grew closer. Her foot caught on a tree root and she stumbled forward. Trent caught her before she fell face-first on top of Josiah.

"I can't keep this pace." She blinked back threatening tears. Her emotions were all over the place today. Just the thought of her unstable feelings made her want to cry.

"We'll slow down before one of us gets hurt. If I have to shoot it, I will, but running isn't worth the risk." He wrapped his arm around her shoulders. "Can you keep walking?"

"Not much choice, is there?" She leaned on him for added strength. Walking was one thing but running up a mountain wasn't in her recovery orders.

They emerged from the pine trees into an open field. The squealing faded, and she released the breath she'd held. The sun rose higher, but the temperatures remained cool. Her head spun for a moment and stopped.

"My head spins now and then." She pressed her hand against her forehead. "And I'm getting a headache."

"You're exhausted, dehydrated and half starved. We're still climbing and getting into higher altitudes. Not as high as the trail, though."

She struggled with each breath. Carrying extra weight hadn't changed much. Inside or out, she still had Josiah with her.

"If you could go anywhere in the world, where would you go?" he asked.

She had a feeling he was trying to distract her from the danger surrounding them. "Someday, I'd like to go to Alaska to hike with all those grizzlies."

He glanced back. "Oh, you know about the grizzlies?"

"I do watch nature shows. I'm not totally ignorant."

"I think you must be pretty knowledgeable to own your own business." He hefted himself up on a rock that blocked their path and offered his hand.

She welcomed the help and stepped up beside him. "Evidently, I'm not as smart as I thought. I'm wondering if Nick lost my business in his shenanigans. His name was on the deed, too. Guess I'll find out when I get home and check the damages to our finances."

"What will you do after you get home, besides bury your husband, care for Josiah and monitor your business?"

"Get back in church and get on with my life. What about you?"

"Hmm, living alone isn't all it's made out to be. Think I'll get back in the dating scene and see what God has planned. I even considered asking you out."

"But what about your demanding job? I thought it consumed your time?"

"It does if I allow it."

Her heart pounded in her ears. Each step up the wooded trail a chore. Had she heard him right? She'd ponder the idea. Dreams of home, a nice shower, clean clothes, a hot meal and her own bed danced in her head, that was, after being released from the hospital. *Focus. One foot in front of the other.*

"So where would you go if you could go anywhere? Back to the mountains?" She rolled her eyes and expected a camping response.

"Italy or England. Traveling abroad has always interested me."

"That's shocking. I assumed you'd return to the forest."

"I live close enough to the mountains that I can visit whenever I want. Exploring new territories overseas sounds intriguing."

"I've always wanted to go to Italy. Maybe some… ouch, ouch, ouch!" She danced in place, slapping at her leg.

Rex backed away, barking.

Trent spun. "What's wrong?"

"Something bit me." She slapped as her leg.

"Fire ants." He brushed the ants off her leg. You must have stepped on a fire ant mound. An army of them will crawl up and all sting at one time. It's going to hurt and make red welts around your ankle, then it will start itching or burning. Let's find a place to stop. I've got hydrocortisone cream in my first aid kit."

She slapped at her leg again and stomped her feet. Heat rose to her face. "Are they still on me? Will they attack Josiah?" She shivered. "How am I supposed to see the ground with all these overgrown weeds? Why aren't you bothered by any of this stuff? Why am I always the one causing problems?"

He sat her on a stump. She jumped to her feet and searched the ground and around the stump. "Is it safe? Is something else going to bite me?" She lost her balance and her breathing increased. "I... I can't breathe."

Rex drew closer and stood, watching her.

"Sit down. You're hyperventilating. Don't want you to pass out." He rambled through his bag and pulled out a small paper bag. "Here, hold this over your mouth and focus on breathing slow and steady for a few breaths. Six to twelve is recommended."

He untied the baby wrap.

"Giving you a break." He lifted Josiah into his arms. "We're good. Breathe. Focus. Relax."

"My heart is racing. Is it the altitude?" Concern edged in a panic attack. Would she die up here?

Trent held her baby in one arm like a football while he applied the medication on the bites with a small gauze pad. Her leg burned. Felt like two armies of ants zeroed in on her one leg. The itching intensified. She had to scratch it. He moved her hand away.

"It's going to burn and itch for about ten minutes. Give it time to calm down. Keep your hands off." He pointed to the bag. "Use the bag again. Controlled breathing is what you need. Breathe in slowly through your nose. Then, gradually blow out through your mouth. Focus on that pattern until you feel you're in control again."

She complied. Every vein in her body throbbed.

He stood in front of her, patting Josiah on the back.

"You're having an anxiety attack and your stress level is over the top plus you're totally out of your element. You wouldn't know it, but I can't stand tight, enclosed places. When that happens, I must focus on what's going on around me and not the position or size of the space I'm in. Sounds nonsensical, but it helps."

She eased the bag from her face. "Think I'm better now."

He took her chin in his hand and tilted her face up toward his. Was he going to kiss her again? Did she want him to? No. Not right now.

"Your color is better. You were pale for a few minutes."

"I'm so embarrassed." Her face warmed. He wasn't getting romantic during an awkward, pivotal moment. He took care of her, making sure she recovered. Never had she been this much of an imposition to anyone. Her self-reliant, independent nature had her caring for herself, twenty-four-seven. "Give me a minute. I know we need to keep moving."

"We're not punching a time clock." He handed her a water bottle. "Have a drink and rest a minute."

"But I want to get home before I collapse. I don't know how much longer I can keep moving."

Concern for Brooke's health had Trent unnerved. If she'd suffered nightmares before the weekend started, they'd most likely get worse after her rescue. She thought of herself as weak, but his evaluation noted her overall condition. Double trauma with the death of her husband and delivering a baby in the woods, fearful and uncertain extenuating circumstances, killers chasing after her, and protecting her baby. Who wouldn't react similarly or worse?

She pushed to her feet and stood, taking in several deep breaths and exhaling. "I'm feeling better. If you'll hand me Josiah and tie the wrap, we can continue our journey."

"Okay, if you're sure. We can stay here and make camp. Rescuers will just have to find us." He chewed on his lip. They needed to keep moving.

If he had to guess the distance to the ranger's station, he'd say they were about three miles out. He'd followed the direction of the compass, but they were in unfamiliar territory, so there was no way to know for sure. If he were alone, he could make it to the top of the mountain where he'd get a phone signal, and back down in about two-and-a-half hours. Maybe sooner.

Leaving her wasn't an option. In her present state, she'd have a nervous breakdown if he mentioned moving on without her. So close to the top and yet too far away. He'd never leave her and Josiah alone. Not now, and not after they were rescued. If she allowed him in her life.

"It's tempting to stay put, but I don't want to hinder our progress any more than I already have." She tugged the scrunchie out and repositioned it. "Are you ready? There, I beat you to it. You didn't have to ask me." Her smile hadn't convinced him of her recovery, but at least her countenance had improved.

He tied the baby wrap around her and held her shoulders. Her droopy, sad eyes gripped him. "If you need to stop, say so."

He regretted taking her and Josiah away from the waterfall. Such uncertainty in staying there. Once he built another shelter, he wouldn't force her to leave again until her strength returned. She needed rest worse than he realized.

"I will." Weakness emanated from her voice.

He tossed his bag onto his back and took her hand. "Walk beside me, not behind me. We're in this together."

Her hand squeezed his without another word. Josiah's little face lay against her chest and tilted upward. He slept peacefully.

Trent purposefully slowed his pace and tried making the hike seem more like a leisurely stroll. His job kept him in staunch, on guard mode, searching with Rex for the lost, not knowing the outcome. While he remained in recovery mode with Brooke, compassion settled him. He'd get her and Josiah to safety, regardless, and pray she'd be receptive to going out with him and possibly, a future together.

"Step over that puddle of water. There are several holes around here."

Rex trotted ahead and occasionally looked back at him.

"You never finished telling me about your grandfather," he said.

"He loved the outdoors, like you, and every time I visited him, he always had something for me. Similar to the way you're constantly making sure I have food and water." Her voice steady, but weak. "A balloon, ballerina shoes, a book, candy or popsicles. He lived a few blocks from our house, so I saw him often. When I turned fifteen, he gave me my grandmother's Bible. I loved the ground he walked on.

"What about your grandparents?" She glanced his direction.

He slowed and helped her step over a few tree roots. "They're not around anymore either. I spent my summers exploring their farm, building forts in the hayloft against my pop's wishes, fishing with a cane pole in the pond and disappearing in the woods behind their house. Grandma had a cowbell hanging outside the back door. She rang when she wanted me to come inside."

"Sounds like you grew up playing in the forest."

"I did. Have a lot of fond memories. Guess that's why I love hiking and camping."

Rex stilled, looked back, then to the trees, and growled.

"What is it, boy?" Trent studied his canine's actions.

Brooke's hand tightened around his. "Now what?"

"Not an animal. He hears something else." He stopped with her by his side. "Listen."

"Rescue?" Her voice rose an octave.

Rex barked and wagged his tail. Trent shortened the leash and kept his K-9 by his side.

The hair on Trent's arms lifted at the sound of male voices. He hid her behind a tree and waited. The voices weren't familiar. Different people? They appeared from the tree line ahead. Two older men and a younger man. Relief swept over him.

The guys walked toward them. Rex growled. "Quiet. Sit."

"Hey, nice day for a hike," one of the older men said.

"What brings you this way? You're off the beaten path." Trent studied them. They seemed harmless enough, laughing and talking with a backpack on each of their backs.

"Yeah, we've hiked all the main trails many times. Thought we'd venture out and see where it takes us," the second older man said. "Keeping our compass handy so we don't get lost."

"Any idea how far it is to the ridge from here?" Trent pointed toward the mountain.

"Couple of miles if you go over the top. Tough incline, though. Going this way, around the mountain valley, you're probably looking at two and a half to three miles." The first older man pointed to Brooke. "Newborn, aye? Hope you don't have far to go. You're looking rather whipped."

Brooke opened her mouth, but Trent spoke up. "You guys have a satellite phone? We need food, water and a rescue team."

"Yep. Never come out here without it," the younger man responded.

"Mind if we borrow it and call for help? Broke mine a couple of days ago." Trent squeezed Brooke's hand.

"Sure. Anything else we can do?" The younger guy slung his backpack off his shoulder and started unzipping it.

Shots fired, pinging the surrounding trees. Trent's arm stung.

"What kook is out there shooting at people?" the younger guy yelled as he grabbed his bag and ran.

Trent pushed Brooke back behind a large tree with Rex at their feet. He pulled his pistol and peered around the trunk in search of movement. Something warm soaked his sleeve. He wiped at the sting. Blood.

Brooke's hand grabbed his wrist. "Oh, no. You're bleeding?"

No time to tend to a wound. It hadn't incapacitated him. He'd check it when their threat subsided. The three new guys disappeared down the mountain with their satellite phone in tow. His heart plummeted. Help was a phone call away and now it was gone. Surely those guys would call and report the incident.

Another shot chipped bark off the tree. Trent blinked when pieces slapped his face. The near misses unnerved him. If only they were closer. He edged from his cover and spotted the killers still up on the ridge he assumed to be one of the lower points of Redbud Trail. They must have turned around and followed the path until they'd gone far enough to spot them again. The distance between them grew closer, but still out of physical reach.

He refused to shoot back from this distance. With limited bullets, he'd save his rounds for a clearer, sure shot. If help didn't arrive soon, he'd have to defend himself and protect Brooke and Josiah.

His head spun. Brooke had released her hold on his wrist and hadn't spoken another word. Her eyes were closed, and her arms wrapped around her infant. "Hey, are you okay?"

"Focusing on breathing and not freaking." She said in a monotone voice. "You're hurt."

"I'm fine."

"You've got this, right?"

Rex whined and nudged his hand. Trent patted his head, then touched Brooke's shoulder.

"Yes. I've got this." Not sure what the next encounter would entail when they met the killers face-to-face.

"Where did the guy with the satellite phone go?" She cut her eyes up at him.

"They ran down the mountain. I'm sure they'll call and report the incident."

"Then, help is on the way, and we'll get to go home today."

"We're getting closer with each step." He couldn't guarantee rescue today. His hand swiped over the wound again, and he tugged at the rip to look at it. The bullet grazed his upper arm and took a small chunk of flesh with it.

"The killers are running. They've figured out how to reach us. We'll proceed unless you need to stop." His muscles tightened. Moving around in the open would put them in a vulnerable state.

He dropped his bag and retrieved the first aid kit. "Here. Wipe my arm down with this alcohol pad, rip that small antibiotic ointment package open and apply—"

"I know how to do this. Relax your arm." She did as he requested. Located a Band-Aid and pulled it tight across the wound. She used the only small wrap in the kit and wrapped it around his arm. "Does it hurt?" She closed the kit and dropped it in his bag.

He stared into her eyes. "Do I really need to answer that question? Feels like a bullet grazed my arm and someone put a branding iron to it. Come on. Let's get out of here."

Chapter Twelve

Brooke's insides trembled. The casual stroll had only lasted a short time. Trent's tight grip squished her fingers together. He dragged her behind him at a fast pace, determined to get them to safety. Her already weak body rebelled. Light-headedness had her mind swirling and intensified her headache. Weakness hit her knees and the bites on her leg burned. Not to mention the soreness of those scrapes and bruises on her arms, back and legs. When would it end?

Josiah kicked and wiggled. The bumpy ride upset him. Did Trent know the exact direction of their destination? Any wavering from a direct path could take her over the edge.

"Trent. Stop. I can't keep this pace." She jerked her hand from his grip. "I want to, believe me. I want to go home more than you." She bent and held her knees, dangling Josiah mid-air against her body. She gasped for breath. "I'm not hyperventilating again. I'm done. We've got to stop. My legs won't take me any farther."

She folded her legs and sat on the ground. "Another step and I'll pass out."

Perspiration rolled from her forehead. "You'll literally have to drag me if we have to keep going."

He raked his fingers through his hair and stood over her. He walked circles around her.

"What are you doing?" she asked. "Did you hear me?"

"We're so close. Two more miles, at most." He leaned down and put his hands on his knees and looked into her eyes. "I heard you. There's a grove of trees just a short distance away. I think it would shield us from being spotted from the trail. We can't stay in this spot. It's too open. We need the thick covering of those pine trees."

"Give me some water. I can't move again unless I have something to drink."

When he didn't react, she looked up at him. He shuffled his feet. Rex trotted back and forth with his nose in the air.

"Trent. Please, I need water."

"I hear you, Brooke. I'm not sure we're clear of danger sitting here in the open." He reached his hand toward her. "We can't stop here. It's not safe. Let me help you to those trees."

She bit her lip. Could she even stand?

His fingers wrapped around her hand. He pulled her to her feet. Her knees gave way. He wrapped his muscular arm around her waist. His side grip lifted most of her weight, and her toes barely touched the ground. She made sure Josiah stayed put. Her little guy slept and behaved so well. Oh, the stories she'd tell him when he was old enough to understand.

"You don't have to carry me. You're hurt." Her body flopped around in his semi-jog.

"Getting you and Josiah out of harm's way. Just a few more yards."

How did this doubly wounded K-9 handler muster up the strength to keep going? He hadn't had adequate fluids to sustain him any more than she. Dehydration imprisoned her and threatened Trent. He held back his water intake so she could have more. Where did this selfless guy come from? He and his canine had risked everything for her and Josiah.

Another bullet hit the ground in front of them, kicking up grass and dirt. He didn't slow down. It was as though he'd gulped a double shot of espresso. His grip tightened, and he ran faster up the incline. Pain in her sides throbbed from his death grip. The pine grove drew closer and closer. The incline grew steeper. Trent slowed his pace and carried her deeper into the pine tree copse.

"We should be okay here for a while." He lowered her to her feet.

She faltered and lowered herself to the ground. How much more could her body endure? The dirty ground cried out to her. Lying down sounded like heaven.

"I cannot take another step." Regret hit hard. Breathing grew harder. Her shoulders drooped and her hands covered her face. "God, I can't do this anymore. I need You now, more than ever. Forgive me for my lack of trust in You, in myself and in others. I don't want to die out here. Please send help."

"You're going to be okay. You said God gives strength. He's not going to leave any of us now." Trent tossed the backpack on the ground, retrieved the fabric he'd cut from the abandoned tent he'd stuffed inside and spread it beside her. "Do you have the energy to move over so you're not sitting in pine needles?"

"I think so." Her arms trembled as she pressed her hands on the ground and shuffled onto the fabric. She willed herself to relax and let God's peace calm her. "I'm drained."

"The altitude isn't helping your breathing." He handed her a bottled water. "Drink this."

"You need to drink some, too." Her eyes rolled. "I need to lie down." Weakness crawled over her like a dark cloud. She leaned and lay on her side.

Josiah cried out. She patted his back with the remaining strength she mustered up.

Trent stooped beside her and pushed hair from her face. "Brooke, you didn't drink the water, and you need to feed your baby. Stay awake a little while longer."

"No energy." Her mouth and voice didn't cooperate.

"Don't pass out on me." He sat beside her. His touch assured her she wasn't alone. He lifted her to a sitting position, unwrapped the baby wrap and took Josiah. His movements were like slow motion. Trent laid him in her lap and put the water bottle in her hand, wrapping her fingers around the bottle and putting the water to her lips.

"Take a few swallows."

Little crying squeals forced her to focus. She drank some of the sun-warmed water. Ice-cold water sounded better. The wetness moistened her dry mouth.

"Do you want me to try feeding Josiah some water with Mandy's baby doll bottle?" Trent asked.

"Maybe later. Think I can feed him." *I must. He needs proper nourishment.*

"While you take care of him, I'm going to build a shelter." He stood. "I'm not going far. I'll be in sight. Don't worry."

"Okay. I trust you." Her eyes fought to stay open as she concentrated on feeding her baby. "Putting water in the baby doll bottle might be a good idea in case of an emergency." Her arms shook with weakness. She pondered her condition. Exhaustion ranked over dehydration. Rest and sleep tugged mercilessly.

Her focus landed on Trent out in the distance, gathering long limbs with Rex wandering around unleashed, biting at sticks and dragging them to Trent's side. How could she have made it without him, or either of them? She wouldn't, and Josiah, well, she couldn't think about what the outcome might have been.

His muddy, ripped clothing matched hers. He'd endured more than he bargained for meeting up with her three days ago. Blood stains from gunshot near misses, a bandaged arm, the rugged look of a growing beard and tousled hair.

Were his gentle kisses on her forehead and lips mere moments of emotion caused by Josiah's safe delivery and her need for assurance? She admitted trusting him, but the gnawing question was could she trust herself? Yes. She'd prayed and released it all. God had never failed her. She trusted Him most of all. Her lip quivered.

She lifted her tiny bundle to her shoulder and patted his back. A little burp filled with air and a drizzle of milk rolled from the corner of his mouth. She dabbed his miniature lips with the baby blanket.

Trent marched determined steps toward her with his arms full of limbs. He dropped them a few feet from her and pointed. Rex trotted alongside him and sniffed the ground when he stopped.

"Our shelter for the night." His caring eyes searched her. "How are you feeling?"

"Not as well as you. But being off my feet helps." She blinked back threatening tears. "I know you're as ready to get out of here as I am. The thought of taking another step makes me nauseous. Just take Josiah and the two of you go get help. I'll wait here."

He stiffened. "That's not going to happen. We're all getting out of here together. Sit back and relax or lie back and take a nap. I'm taking care of things."

"You've taken care of everything since the moment we invaded your camp. How can I ever thank you and Rex for saving our lives?" She wiped tears from her face and coddled Josiah.

"No thanks necessary. It's all part of our job, both as search and rescue and survival experience." He chuckled. "Must admit, assisting a pregnant lady running for her life, delivering a baby in the forest and life-and-death survival has elevated our personal learning experiences firsthand."

She forced a grin. *All part of his job.* He'd probably get a medal or an award for his victorious rescue. He deserved it, no doubt. Rex, too. Her post birth hormones ran rampant as she read more into his words than what he'd said. She wanted him in her life if only he didn't work such long hours. He'd mentioned taking her out, but she hadn't graced him with a positive answer.

* * *

"Stand guard, Rex. While I make us a shelter," Trent commanded.

Rex's shrill whine and couple of barks showed he understood. He sniffed each limb Trent lifted and tried dragging a few with his teeth.

"Find a fork in three tall limbs. Clean off the foliage and hook them together in the fork."

"Are you talking to me?" Brooke asked.

"Huh, oh. Talking to myself and trying to remember how to do this."

He stood back and studied his outline. The forks in the branches gave the frame a tripod or triangle effect. He studied the lengths of the sticks and selected some near the same length, ripped off the foliage again, then placed them side by side, in an upright position where they rested against the frame limbs.

"It's coming together." He looked at Brooke, who sat silently watching. Help had to arrive soon. She and Josiah needed medical attention, stat. More than he could give or had resources to give now.

He piled more branches on top of the ones that formed the walls, then dragged green pine branches filled with foliage and placed them on top, forming a roof.

"Not bad, if I say so myself." He placed his hands at his waist and admired his creation. He glanced at Brooke. She lay on her side on the tent fabric, with Josiah beside her.

"Is there anything you can't do?" Her weak voice proved her fatigue.

"Plenty. Like create a four-wheeler or lift us out of here in a helicopter." He scanned the ground.

"What's next?"

"Pine needles make a good padding for the floor."

He scraped his foot along the ground, forming piles of pine needles, then scooped them up and tossed them inside the shelter. He crawled inside, with Rex crowding in beside him, and spread them out. Rex nosed through the needles and sneezed, licked his face then trotted outside.

He backed out into the open. Brooke lay on the tent fabric he needed to place over the pine needles and put the finishing touches on the floor.

I'll get it later. Let her rest.

His dry mouth longed for a drink. He joined her on the ground and located a bottle of water in his backpack. Only two remained. He hadn't spotted a stream nearby, leaving him no choice but to limit his intake so she'd have enough to get by. He'd trained for difficult situations, although this one would go down in the record books. He'd get her out, no doubt. Help wasn't far over the mountain. She and Josiah were his future.

The ground under the pine trees was a blanket of pine needles and dirt. No tall weeds to wrestle with or hidden fire ant mounds. He blew out a long breath and scanned their surroundings. The peaceful aura filled the air as a breeze brushed branches together in the tall trees. Rex lay at his feet.

Calm before the storm? Trent chewed his lip.

Help should arrive soon. Today, tomorrow? Who knew? If her parents reported her missing, his parents reported him missing, with the two encounters with hikers surely word had spread, and search teams were actively looking for them. They weren't far from Red-bud Trail, which would make locating them easier, but posed another problem. The killers.

He patted his sides and confirmed both pistols were still in place. Glanced at Brooke as she slept. Josiah kicked. His eyes wide open. He kicked the blanket off, exposing his miniature feet. His arms reached into the air while his hands formed into fists.

Rex scooted closer and sniffed. Josiah's fist bumped his wet nose. He drew back and watched the tiny human move.

Trent picked him up and held him out in front of his face. Such tiny, delicate features. His little eyes searched, and his mouth opened. He sucked on his fist. Blond hair tossed like feathers in the breeze. Trent's heart warmed. He loved this little guy, and the child wasn't even his. And to think, Brooke named him after her grandfather and after him.

He laid Josiah down in front of him and retrieved a dry homemade diaper and shirt and changed him.

"Good thing I watched Dana change Mandy's diapers. Otherwise, I'd be clueless or clumsy," he whispered.

Josiah seemed content lying on the ground, stretching his legs.

Deep breathing assured Brooke slept soundly. She'd fuss at him if she knew he watched her sleep, but he couldn't take his eyes off her. Several scratches from low-lying limbs left minor cuts on her face. Bruises scattered on the backs of her hands and on her arms. City girl or not, she'd faced her dilemmas honorably.

Josiah stilled, and his eyes closed. Trent covered him with the blanket. What would it be like to have them around all the time? An instant family. Could he handle it? Did he want it? He'd been so troubled by the loss of the preemie that self-doubt and fear encapsulated his reasoning. He'd lost his joy and his ability to make a wise decision about his future.

Brooke forced him to face his fears. He'd doubted God and almost made a decision he would have regretted. Anger strangled the joy he once enjoyed. Leaving or transferring from the K-9 unit no longer muddled his thoughts. He'd remain in his present position at work and might consider taking more classes to become a paramedic. Didn't mean he wouldn't have losses, but he might have a better understanding of how or why they happened. One thing for sure, Brooke helped him realize the preemie's death wasn't his fault, and that God never left his side.

Was Brooke his divine intervention? He raked a hand over his face as the realization hit. He'd prayed before Josiah's birth and God heard him. The weight of doubt and unbelief lifted, and peace filled the void he'd suffered. Such mercy.

Rex nuzzled up to Trent. Trent rubbed his head and patted his sides. "Man's best friend. That's what you are. I've decided I'm not going anywhere."

"Where are you going?" Brooke stirred.

"Nowhere. I'm right here."

"How long have I been asleep?" She pushed to a sitting position and smiled at her baby sleeping in front of Trent. "Has he cried?"

"You slept a couple of hours. I changed his clothes." Trent straightened. "He looks a lot like you."

"Thanks, I think so too." She smiled, stretched her arms in the air and rolled her shoulders. "That felt good. My body feels like a fifty-pound weight is pressing me into the ground. What time is it?"

Trent checked his watch. "It's almost three-thirty in the afternoon. Tomorrow is Tuesday."

"I don't want to hear about tomorrow. The rangers have to find us today." She covered her ears.

"We have to plan ahead. It's good survival skills." His thoughts reeled. Anything could happen at any moment. Rescue, the killers or a wild animal. At this point, he'd shoot whatever wildlife roamed close, so they'd have food. If it drew the killers nearer, he and Rex would deal with them.

"My leg burns and itches." The fiery red welts looked heated and irritated.

"Need to put more hydrocortisone cream on them. It'll help you tolerate the pain." He opened the first aid kit, leaned toward her leg and smoothed on the medication.

"I know it's nice to sit out here in the breeze," he added, "but the shelter isn't as easily spotted as we are out here moving around." He wiped his hands with an alcohol wipe, hopped to his feet and picked Josiah up. "If you can stand for a few minutes, I'll put the fabric on the ground inside today's new home."

"That's really not funny, but I will comply." She pushed to her feet and groaned. "Wow. Is the forest spinning or is it me?"

He walked Brooke over to a tree trunk. "Lean against

the tree while I move the fabric." He handed Josiah to her and waited. "Are you okay to hold him and stand there a minute?"

"I believe so. If it gets worse, I'll just sit down."

Trent crawled inside the shelter and spread out the fabric. He backed out and motioned for Brooke to come, then hopped up, met her midway and took Josiah from her arms.

"Let me hold him while you crawl inside."

She wobbled to the entrance, stooped down and entered.

"Good job." She licked her lips and pressed them together.

His eyes landed on her lips. The urge to kiss her rushed over him. He turned his head and backed away.

"Was it something I said?" she asked.

"Getting the backpack. Need to take inventory and see what food supplies we have left." He scolded himself for thinking about romance in her vulnerable state. Only time, after their rescue, would reveal his genuine feelings. Hers, too. He'd best keep his distance. At least for now.

"My guess is we're nearing the end." She placed Josiah by her side. Tugged the scrunchie from her ponytail and finger combed her long brown hair. She fluffed it with her fingers and pulled it back up into a ponytail.

He joined her in the small space and emptied the bag.

"No more beef jerky. Here's one peanut butter cracker that must have fallen out of the pack, a couple snack-size packages of trail mix, half of an energy bar and Rex's meal substitutes and snacks…"

Rex barked and wagged his tail. Trent tossed him a snack.

"Oh." He unzipped the outer pocket. "I forgot about the berries."

Her eyes brightened. "Yum. Pass me a few." She held her hand out.

"Low on Water. We'll have to ration our intake." He dropped berries in her hand. His dry mouth longed for a gallon of cold water or sweet iced tea. Didn't matter, something cold and wet to take away the dehydration creeping over him.

"If help hasn't arrived by morning, I'll go hunting and find us something more substantial to eat." A big, juicy T-bone sounded tasty. He forced those dreams away. *Focus.*

Chapter Thirteen

Brooke munched on the wild blackberries. The sugar rush helped rejuvenate some of her strength. For how long, she didn't know. She took one sip of water and closed the lid.

"I guess this means we sit and wait." She lifted her eyebrows at Trent and awaited his response.

"That's all we can do at this point." He picked at a pine needle and didn't look up. "You can't keep going. If you collapse and become too weak to take care of Josiah, we're in trouble. I certainly can't feed him."

She blushed. "True on all counts. But, if I do collapse, as you mentioned earlier, you could give him drops of water from Mandy's doll baby bottle. I'm certain we'll be home by tomorrow night."

A howl in the distance sent a shudder through her. She froze and stared at Trent. Rex hopped to his feet and barked.

"Quiet, Rex. They're off in the distance, miles away. Sound travels out here." He waved his hand at her.

"You'll hear them more in some areas than you will in others. We're okay."

"You would tell me the truth, wouldn't you?"

"Didn't you tell me to soften my answers and not tell you everything?" He smiled.

"Yes. I do want the truth, but I don't. Hearing them frightens me."

"There are a lot of sounds in the forest. It's the animals' ways of communicating with each other. For instance, one pack of coyotes may tell another pack that we're sitting ducks right here in…"

"Stop. You're taunting me." She pushed his shoulder, and he winced. "Oh, no, I hit your gunshot wound. I didn't mean to do that. How is it?"

"Sore." He rolled his shoulder.

"Let me check it." She scooted closer and unwrapped the bandage. "It's red and irritated. I need to put more of that antibiotic cream on it."

"Figured as much."

He lifted his arm, and she applied the medication, and rewrapped his arm. Her eyes met with his when he turned and looked at the bandage. Her heart skipped a beat. Right here in the wild, half starved and dehydrated. She wanted his lips pressed against hers.

"Good job. I couldn't have done better myself." Could he read her thoughts?

She jerked back and put the supplies in the first aid kit. He and Rex were doing their job. He said so himself. She'd become one of his jobs. No need to express any more emotions with this handsome K-9 handler.

"As soon as help arrives, I'm certain the doctor will give you an antibiotic." She avoided eye contact. "Truth is, we both need IV fluids and a good solid meal. Josiah needs medical evaluation and whatever else infants need."

Rex curled up beside Trent. He stretched his arm out and ruffled his fur. "She speaks truth, partner. You need a good meal and some nutrition as well. We all could use a good shower and I need a shave. This beard itches and is driving me nuts."

"You don't normally wear a beard?"

"A shadow, sometimes, but not a full beard." He backed out of the shelter.

"Where are you going?" His presence made her feel safe, even if he wasn't interested in her romantically.

"Gotta prepare a place for a fire. We have dried pine trees all around. Since we're on an incline, it's dryer here than most places. All the water drains off fast. It's a hazard and could easily catch the forest on fire if we're not careful."

"Do we have to have one?" Her pulse increased.

"I don't recommend the pitch black of the mountains after dark. We *need* a fire. The temperatures drop, and we'll need the heat. Another reason is nocturnal animals come out and roam. It wouldn't be safe. The flames will help keep them away. Besides, we're not the only campers in the forest. The killers won't necessarily think it's ours. I don't think they would risk moving around at night, but who knows, they did the night you ran into my camp."

"Then, build a big one. All of it makes me nervous." She took in a shaky breath and released it in a huff. No more hyperventilating.

Brooke picked Josiah up and scooted to the opening

of the shelter. Trent cleared a spot close to the doorway. He grabbed a stick and dug a big hole in the ground. Then tossed dried pine needles in the bottom and criss-crossed small sticks above them. He lit a handful of pine needles with the remaining propane and slid them under the sticks, catching the other pine needles on fire.

Heat rose from the hole as flames danced above ground level. His ingenuity impressed her. He could teach Josiah so much with all his skills. Her unstable emotions had her longing for him to hold her in his muscular arms while she rested her head on his shoulder.

"The smoke will help keep mosquitoes away, too." He poked at the flames and added a few larger limbs. "Once the sun starts going down, it's like someone cut the rope holding it up. It plummets fast and before you know it, blackness rules."

"I've never been afraid of the dark, but here in the wilderness, it terrifies me." She kissed Josiah's soft head and pulled the blanket up to shield him from the heat of the fire and observed Trent. "Have you and Rex rescued anyone in these mountains before?"

He sat on the ground opposite the campfire. "Rex. Come." Rex turned circles before he lay down beside him. Trent hooked the leash back on his collar and looped the handle on his wrist.

She could admire him all night if she weren't so tired.

"Only the outer realm. Most of our search and rescue is in the city." Trent ruffled Rex's fur. "Helping people is what it's all about."

"Like me. You're just doing your job." Her head

pounded. Why had she snapped at him? He didn't deserve it. Was she thinking of herself as one of his jobs?

"Exactly. Uh, no, not in the sense you're insinuating." He grew serious. "True, you've given us more experience than all the cases we've had in the past few years, but never would I have imagined finding the missing link in my life in the forest. Finding you."

She looked at him and her vision blurred. He moved closer and felt her forehead.

"Brooke, look at me." His voice filtered through her ringing ears. "Talk to me."

Her head spun.

"I… I don't feel well."

"You're burning up with fever."

Everything went black.

Brooke fell sideways. Trent caught her and caught Josiah before she dropped him. He eased her down on the floor.

"Come on, Brooke. This can't be happening." Josiah stretched, and the blanket opened. Trent adjusted the blanket and laid him down. He turned back to Brooke and pushed loose strands of hair from her face. Perspiration beaded on her forehead.

A wet cloth. What could he use? He ripped the tail off his shirt and poured a small amount of water on it and put it to her forehead. Would it help? Cold water would be better. A cold pack. Had he spotted a small one in the first aid kit?

Supplies spilled on the floor as he shook the backpack. He scooped the kit up and flipped it open. Yes. A small instant cold pack lay in the mesh holder of the lid.

He jerked it out and squeezed the pack until it popped. He shook it vigorously. Instant cold chilled his hand.

"Don't do this to me, Brooke. We have to work together to get out of here. Josiah needs you. I need you." He wrapped the ice pack in the torn piece of his shirt and placed it on her head. "Come on. Wake up."

His heart thundered in his chest. He checked her pulse. Slow but steady. The circles under her eyes confirmed dehydration, but what else had her unconscious?

She moaned.

"I'm right here. You're going to make it." He patted her cheeks. "Can you hear me?"

Rex reclined in the shelter doorway.

Trent leaned back, took in a deep breath and exhaled slowly. *Calm down and think.*

Complications with childbirth? Too much running? Lack of fluids? Exhaustion? All were possibilities. He checked the fire ant bites around her ankle. The hydrocortisone cream had helped, and the welts didn't look too irritated. Couldn't be them.

If he'd paid attention to all her complaints, he might know what caused her to pass out. She'd complained about a headache but hadn't said how bad. Her muscles ached and grew weak. He assumed her occasional moodiness came from being pregnant and having a baby. She grumbled about being drained and had every right. His energy level wasn't up to par either.

Trent paused. All her complaints pointed to sheer exhaustion. Lack of food and liquids only intensified the symptoms. He picked up a full bottle of water and shifted his position, so Brooke's head rested on his leg.

The ice pack fell off. He held it against her head and monitored her and Josiah.

"Please, little man. Don't get hungry right now," he whispered.

The fire needed more sticks. Leaving Brooke and the baby to take care of it gnawed at him. He'd grown close to them. Closer than he'd imagined.

"Rex, drop some sticks in the fire." It was worth a chance. He mused.

Rex hopped to his feet and came inside the shelter with a stick in his mouth. "Thanks, but I wanted you to put it in the fire." He patted Rex's side.

Rex walked slowly out the doorway with the stick still in his mouth. He looked back at Trent. Had he understood?

"That's it. Drop it."

He dropped it and it rolled in. "Good job."

Brooke's heavy breathing assured him she slept hard. He slid her head to the ground and moved Josiah closer to her. The fire needed more attention than Rex understood. He stepped out into the cool of the night. The light from the flames grew dim. He tossed more pine needles into the hole and the flames came to life. A few more sticks and three thicker branches had it crackling and popping.

A half-full bottle of water still sat in his bottle holder at his waist. He retrieved it and the remaining blackberries. The juicy flavor stirred his tastebuds. Small sips of water helped wash it all down.

Could she hear him if he talked? Was she unconscious or asleep? Big difference.

"Brooke, I finished the blackberries. If you insist, I'll

see if I can find more in the morning." Her breathing grew less heavy. "We have a full moon tonight. You'll be happy to know that when there's a full moon, some of the nocturnal animals stay put because there's too much light. At least, that's what I've heard. Elk become more active during that time, though."

Her hand moved. She pulled the ice pack from her forehead. He eased to her side and picked Josiah up as he wiggled and stretched his arm out from under the blanket. Tiny fingers found Trent's hand and clutched on.

Trent studied the miniature fingers. His heart squeezed. He could handle an instant family. His eyes fell on Brooke. She moved her foot and turned her head.

"Are you awake?" He asked as quietly as he could.

Her lips parted. "What happened?" Her eyes remained closed.

"Your body is so exhausted that you passed out." He held her hand. "I should have listened to you all those times you told me how tired you were."

"Not your fault. We had to keep moving." Her words came out slow. "I'm so thirsty."

He placed Josiah beside her and put the full water bottle in her hand.

"Can you sit up and drink some water?" Her head didn't feel as warm. The ice pack helped cool her down.

He scooted close so she could lean against him. The fire popped but seemed under control. Rex lay in the doorway.

"Here, I took the cap off the water bottle. Take a drink."

Her eyes opened, and she gulped water.

"Not too fast. Just a swallow at a time." He smoothed his hand over her hair and kissed her on the head. "Nothing a good night's rest won't cure."

She tilted her head and looked up at him. His heart jumped into his throat. He leaned down and brushed a soft kiss across her lips. "I'm glad you're awake enough to get a drink. You had me going for a minute."

She sat up abruptly. "Josiah."

Trent touched her arm and pulled her back against his chest. "He's right here in my arms, just like you. I'm taking care of you both. Take another drink. You need to get more rest, but you should probably feed your little man first."

She sat upright and drank more water. "Put the lid back on and I'll take him. Probably needs changing." Weakness dripped from her voice.

"I'll get out of the way and give you some privacy and more room." Trent scooted to the opening, stood and stepped outside. He sat by the fire with Rex by his side and stared at the full moon.

More coyote howls and an occasional hooting of an owl interrupted the silence. All of them natural sounds of mountain life. His heart warmed at the thought of Brooke and Josiah staying around after rescue arrived. Could she see herself joining him on a few camping trips in the future?

He thumped at the branch made tent. "Knock, knock. Can I come in now?"

"Sure. We're finished."

He stepped inside as she wrapped her bundle in Mandy's blue blanket, kissed him and lay down on her side, cuddling with him, and fell asleep without another word. Beautiful. Inside and out. What a perfect display of unconditional love. He slipped out of the tent and cut his eyes up toward the sky. *Thank you.*

Who cared if she didn't enjoy camping? She was caring, loving and giving. He could commit his life to someone like her, if she felt the same about him.

He picked up a few more sticks and placed them in the fire. Relief that she had come out of her stupor relaxed him. He froze. The realization of her comment about her and Josiah being one of his jobs hit him. She'd totally misunderstood what he said. He thought he'd clarified, but she wasn't feeling well. She may not remember what he'd said.

If she hadn't been sleeping, he'd make things right. She needed her rest. He did, too. He checked his watch. Midnight would be here in another hour. Another day on the horizon. Certain search and rescue halted at dusk. They'd reconvene and start again at daybreak. Only this time, the men with the satellite phone should have given the search party a general location of where they were last seen.

With little water and no food, they wouldn't make it much longer. Trent would have no choice but to shoot a rabbit or a deer or an elk for food. He rubbed his eyes. Shooting would only draw the killers closer.

He shuffled around and stretched out on the ground at the door of the shelter. Rex lay at his head.

His sleeping bag would have been nice about now. He placed his head on his backpack and crossed his arms. Yawned, and closed his eyes.

If a bear or wild hog or coyote found their camp,

they'd have to go through him and Rex before they could get to Brooke and Josiah. He'd keep his word, regardless the dangers, and protect them with his life.

Chapter Fourteen

Brooke lay cuddled up with her newborn. She lifted her head and spotted Trent and Rex sleeping at the doorway. They blocked the door. She enjoyed having him around and had grown to like him a lot. He'd admitted he was a workaholic. She didn't want someone who'd never be home. Besides, he said it was his job to rescue her. She refused to be a number in anyone's work log book.

She rested her head back on the ground. The hooting of the owl sounded familiar. Her breath caught when several coyotes howled. They barked and growled, and the sound of them fighting unnerved her. Trent said they were far away. He seemed to be sure. Guess after all his hiking trips, he had the experience and knowledge.

Her heart ached for her parents and sisters. Not knowing her whereabouts would have them beside themselves with grief. Same with Trent's family. Tears dripped on the shelter floor.

Please send help tomorrow.

The sound of a loud huff sent chills up her spine.

She froze. Rex hadn't lifted his head or barked. Had she imagined it? Footsteps at the back of the shelter. She withheld a scream. Neither Trent nor Rex moved. Would the creature rip the walls down and reach in and grab her? Her imagination went wild.

Trent stirred and Rex lifted his head. The footsteps ran until she didn't hear them anymore. Why hadn't they heard them?

"Are you awake?" she whispered.

Trent sat up and peeked inside. "Yep. What's wrong?"

"There were footsteps behind us. Didn't you hear them?"

"I saw an elk go by, but that's all."

Her shoulders relaxed. He hadn't slept through the animal's approach.

"Relax," Trent whispered. "Go back to sleep. Rex and I are watching out for you."

"Did you hear the coyotes fighting?" The idea of being out in the wilderness and feeling like bait to whatever came her way sent a shiver over her. She preferred a cabin. Even the deserted one would do.

"Yeah, I heard them, too. Quit worrying. I have Rex and two pistols. We're safe."

She bit her lip. Could she sleep now? She had to try. She closed her eyes. Crickets played their sonnet and lulled her back to sleep.

Birds chirping woke her. The dim light of dawn glowed outside. Trent sat by the fire, chewing on a pine needle and petting Rex. Picture perfect. A K-9 and his handler.

He'd kissed her briefly last night. Seemed every

time they kissed, it always happened during an emotional moment. Didn't matter. She enjoyed his kisses and longed for more.

She sat up and stretched her arms, capturing the attention of both Trent and Rex. Trent smiled and Rex beat his tail against the ground.

"Good morning." He looked around. "Join us. We're enjoying a beautiful morning."

Brooke scooped Josiah off the floor and scooted to the door of the shelter. She pushed hair from her face and tugged the scrunchie out. Hair fell over her shoulders.

"How are you feeling this morning? Did you rest?"

She covered her mouth and yawned. "I'll know when I actually stand up. Will you hold Josiah?"

He jumped to his feet, and she handed him over, then pushed to her feet. The weight of her body weakened her legs. If she moved around, would they gain more strength? She slowly paced a few steps.

"I got some broken sleep. Being off my feet all night helped, but I can tell you now, I'm not up to hiking today. My legs may collapse at any moment."

He took her arm with his free hand. "Come back and sit. I don't need you passing out on me again."

"I barely remember what happened last night. Did you put something cold on my forehead?"

"I found an instant ice pack in the first aid kit. You had a fever."

"It sure felt good."

He sat beside her on the ground. A baby in his arms looked natural. Not just any baby, but her baby. "The search party should have regrouped at daybreak and resumed their search. Help may be here sometime today."

"You wouldn't just tell me that to make me feel better, would you?" She studied his expression.

"Never." He lifted his eyebrows. "You want the truth, right?"

"Of course. I may not like the answer." She finger-combed her hair and put the scrunchie back in. Her long ponytail bounced against her back. "When we were hiking I said not to tell me the whole truth, but I didn't mean it like that. I just didn't want to know what dangers lay ahead. I was stressed enough. So, yes, definitely. I always want the truth."

Trent looked down at the bundle in his arms. His hand looked like a giant against Josiah's. She admired the gentle way he held her son and turned him around, facing her. Rex walked over and licked her baby's head.

"If I had your phone, I'd take a picture of you with him to add to your collection of rescues and upping your successes." Her heart ached at the thought of being a number on Trent's shelf.

He shuffled to his feet, holding Josiah with one hand. In a moment's time, he sat next to her and leaned close. "Why do you think you're just a number to me?"

Warmth rushed to her face. "You said yourself that this is what you and Rex do. It's your job."

He laid Josiah in his lap and cupped both sides of her face with his hands. His thumb touched her lips. Her breath hitched. "Let me clarify. Search and rescue are what Rex and I do for a living. It *is* our job, but in no way are you and your son a number added into my book."

"I…" She searched for the right words.

He lifted his hand and put one finger on her lips. "Hear me out. You and Josiah stumbled into my camp and turned my hiking trip upside down. Even with your city-girl ways, the sudden trauma didn't take you down. You've endured more than any one human ever should. And yet, after running for three days, you never gave up. With a baby in tow, you've shown more endurance and determination than I gave you credit."

"I would do anything for my baby's safety." Tears pooled. She blinked them back.

"Exactly. On top of all the dangers, you've faced your fears and forced me to face mine." He kissed her forehead. "I'm a better man because of you." He drew closer. "My outlook on life has taken on a whole new meaning and I have a renewed sense of confidence in my job. Having you by my side brings out the best in me."

Her heart thundered in her chest. One of his hands slid to the back of her neck. He brushed his lips across hers. Softly. Tantalizing. One hand shifted and rested on her side. His lips moved to the nape of her neck, and warm breath sent tingling to her toes.

Don't stop.

His lips found hers again. Tender, smooth. Muscular arms wrapped around her and pulled her closer. His kiss deepened. She gave in to his embrace and put her arms around his neck. How could she have feelings this deep for someone she'd met just days ago?

Rex whined and nudged between them, breaking up the intensity of the moment.

She steadied herself and caught her breath. *Wow.* Her small world soared with wonderment. The dog didn't bother her being so close, and his handler had mesmerized her.

"Rex. You have poor timing." The canine licked his face. Rex's tail wagged and he back-stepped, barking in a playful gesture.

Josiah let out a squeal and sucked on his fist.

"I should feed him." She reached over and took her bundle into her arms. His little mouth searched for food. The temperature inside the shelter proved warmer than out in the open, but offered feeding privacy. From where she sat, Trent and Rex stayed within her view.

Josiah clutched her finger. Her perfect baby. So delicate. Admiration warmed her and for a moment she forgot her location. Trent's passion came through his kisses and caring ways. Regardless of his positive attributes, with his long hours, he'd never be there to teach Josiah to play ball or make a campfire. She didn't want a part-time dad for him.

Rex barked again. He and Trent danced around like two children, jumping at each other, then rolling on the ground. Their playfulness and Trent's laughter had her giggling. Where had this peaceful, fun moment come from?

Trent hopped up and dusted off his pants, then plopped down and zipped open the backpack. He took two swallows of water before filling Rex's water bowl. The half-empty bottle disappeared back inside the bag.

She pursed her lips and studied him. How could he continue surviving on less water? He shared with Rex and kept pushing water on her. She depended on him for protection and had learned some of Rex's actions that warned of approaching danger. Once she arrived home, could she see herself without either of them? Hardly.

Josiah burped and fell asleep. Brooke swaddled him tighter in the blue blanket and laid him on the rough green fabric flooring. She stepped outside the shelter and stretched her back. The weakness in her legs pulsated. How much longer before help arrived?

Trent patted and ruffled his canine's head and ears. Enjoying a moment of playfulness with Rex always put him in a good mood. He glanced at Brooke when she stepped from the shelter. She'd left Josiah on the floor. A change in her perspective of the forest or tired arms? Both, maybe?

His heart yearned for more one-on-one alone time with her. Preferably tasting her lips. Her closeness sent electrical charges through him. He shook off the urge to scoop her into his arms again and forced himself back into survival mode.

If he wanted more water, he'd have to leave their small camp and search for a stream, river, water hole, something. Her body suffered enough already after having a baby.

He rolled his head in circles to relax his neck. The thick pine trees added adequate shelter from the sun and visibility from Redbud Trail. The altitude held temperatures at a tolerable level, but could some of Brooke's dizziness be coming from altitude as well? He rubbed his beard.

Rex jumped to his feet. His ears perked up, and he barked. Trent investigated the trees.

"Quiet." He threw his hand out. Rex obeyed.

"What is it?" Brooke stepped beside him and touched his arm.

"Do you hear it?"

"Hear what? You're scaring me."

"Helicopters. They're looking for us." He spun and scooped her into his arms and turned circles.

"But they can't see us under these thick trees."

"They often use infrared cameras and drones." He set her down. "It won't be long, but until then, we still need water and food."

"I can wait." Her weak eyes sparkled. "This is so encouraging. Help really is on the way."

He had to admit, the sounds of those choppers sure lifted his spirits. No telling how far away they'd have to go to land. He searched his brain, trying to remember where he'd seen an open field. If the ranger's station was only two miles away, they'd most likely land there. Which meant it would take help about an hour and a half or two hours.

"How will they get us out of here if I can't walk these inclines?" Her face switched gears, and the smile faded.

"Brooke, these are professionals. They've experienced many types of rescues from cliff-hanging rescues to weary, dehydrated hikers." He squeezed her shoulders. "They won't have any problems getting you back to the choppers."

"But will they carry me or put me on a stretcher or what? What about Josiah?"

"Don't worry. When they arrive, they'll assess our condition, and may start IV fluids immediately, or they may opt to wait until we're out of the forest. You won't have to walk. They'll have a basket stretcher called a litter. You and Josiah can ride in it while they carry you out. I'm sure your family has already informed them of your situation. The last hikers we saw probably updated them on rescue location and conditions."

Trent picked up a stick and threw it. Rex darted after it and brought it back, then dropped the stick at his feet. "Good job." He tossed it a few more times, reeling in the excitement and expectation of a successful rescue.

"Will they let me carry Josiah?" Her eyes wide and trying to understand how it would all take place. He held back a smile. Her planning and organizational skills worked overtime figuring out the rescue procedures.

"Yes. They will let you carry your baby, or I can carry him. It's up to you."

Trent squatted by the backpack and unzipped the side pocket. "Here, Rex."

Rex trotted to him, wagging his tail.

"Better put your K-9 police vest on. Wouldn't want anyone assuming you're a house pet."

Brooke disappeared inside the shelter and emerged with her baby. The anticipation of rescue filled her face. She stared into the depths of the forest and bounced the infant in her arms nervously.

He sat and gathered the last of the trail mix from the pocket of his bag and set out the remaining two half bottles of water.

"May as well have a seat. They won't be here for a while. Don't want to get too worked up over it just in case rescue takes longer."

She spun. "Don't talk like that. I've been saying for

three days that we've got to get out of here. I'm not adding a fourth day."

He understood her frustration and couldn't blame her. As much as he loved the trails, going home sounded great.

"Munch on this trail mix and let's enjoy the remaining time we have together in the wilderness." He eyed her, keeping a check on her mood and health.

"Do you still hear the helicopters?" Her tone softened.

"No. They've landed already." He tossed a peanut in his mouth. The salty flavor reminded him of the meals he'd missed. His mouth watered. What he wouldn't give for an ice-cold glass of tea.

"Once we're out of here, I'll never take life for granted." She put a raisin in her mouth and chewed slowly. "I've been so busy running my bakery that I've neglected visiting my parents as often as I used to. Now that I have some dependable employees, I may cut my hours back so I can stay home and be the mom Josiah deserves."

"It's okay to work, you know." His job required his full attention, well, during work hours or when there was an emergency after hours.

"True, but I have him to think about. I don't want to miss the first time he lifts his head or the first time he crawls or walks or says mama. In the last years of our marriage, Nick was never at home. I don't want to get so caught up in my job that I neglect having time with my child, and if I ever remarry, I want him to share quality time with Josiah as well. I want a family."

Rex jumped to his feet and growled. The hair on his back raised. Trent got up.

A deer dashed past them and disappeared in the woods. Rex eyed the deer, but his head quickly turned back toward the woods at the side of the tent. A shuffling sound had Trent lifting the pistol from its holster.

"Brooke, get inside the shelter until I know what's approaching."

"Is it them?" Her voice shook in a whisper.

"Shhh. I don't know." He touched her back as she ducked inside the shadows of the tent.

Rex took a few steps forward. He looked back at Trent for instructions with his head and ears held high.

A twig snapped. Trent checked around one side of the tent, turned and eased to the other side. His mouth went dry. Something wasn't right and Rex knew it.

Two of the killers jumped into the open. Both holding guns. Trent's adrenaline exploded. Instantly, Rex dove for one bearded man holding a weapon and knocked him into the other bearded man. Rex held his hostage by the throat. A shot fired. Trent tackled the second bearded man, forcing him to drop his weapon and almost dropped his. They rolled on the ground. The bearded man threw a punch and hit Trent's jaw. Trent flipped the man sideways and jumped to his feet.

The man came at him, but Trent punched him in the gut, then in the face, knocking him off his feet. He didn't want to shoot unless forced to do so.

The third man stepped out from behind the tent, just as the bearded man he'd knocked down grabbed his gun off the ground and fired another shot at him.

Trent dropped and rolled on the ground and shot

back, hitting the bearded man in the knee, right where he'd aimed. The man dropped his gun again and fell to the ground, moaning and holding his leg. Trent pointed his pistol at the third man who held his hands in the air. He scooped the other weapon off the ground.

"I wouldn't make any sudden moves if I were you." Trent motioned with his weapon. "Sit down." He and Rex had subdued the three men, but he didn't have anything to tie them up with. How could he manage them and keep Brooke and Josiah safe?

A rush of stomping feet caught Trent's attention. Rangers and sheriff's deputies flooded their small camp and apprehended two of the killers while Trent tugged on Rex's collar. "Back. Stop. Back."

He let go and backed away, growling.

"Good, boy." Trent held Rex's collar tight. Rex wanted another encounter with the guy, but he pulled him back.

A deputy rushed over and handcuffed the smooth-talking man. Another sheriff's deputy gathered the weapons and placed them in evidence bags.

"Clear." One ranger shouted as they turned to take the cuffed men away. Two on foot and one on a gurney called a litter.

"Hey, wait. Bring the beardless guy over here." Trent tugged him in front of the shelter. "Brooke, recognize this man?"

She slowly peeked out of the tent. A gasp escaped, and her eyes widened. "Parker? You? Why? I thought you were Nick's friend. How could you kill him in cold blood?"

"He owed me." Parker spat on the ground.

"So, you know this guy?" Trent asked.

"Yes. He's my neighbor." She looked at Trent, then back at Parker. "How could you threaten my baby? I don't understand." Tears rolled down Brooke's cheeks.

Trent fumed. He shoved him back to the ranger before his emotions got the best of him and he punched the guy.

Medics rushed into their camp. Trent blew out a huff and pointed toward the shelter. "They're inside."

"They?" The tall medic looked inside, then turned back at Trent. "You delivered a baby out here?"

"Yep. Now it's time to get them help. She's too weak to hike any farther."

"No problem." The two medics ducked and attempted entering, but they both wouldn't fit.

Brooke eased outside and wobbled. "Is it safe for me to come out now?"

"You bet, young lady." The older ranger took her arm and helped her stand. "Who have you got here?"

Trent squared his shoulders and grinned. Brooke caught him staring at her.

"This is Josiah Trent Chandler, born at 2:42 p.m. on Sunday, August eighth." She beamed. "Delivered by K-9 handler Trent Williston."

"Congratulations, to both of you." He turned to Brooke. "Why don't you sit down and let the paramedics get some vitals on you and your newborn."

Brooke complied. They assessed her condition and looked Josiah over. His little arms reached upward, and his legs kicked. Squeaky cries announced his disapproval of being exposed.

The ranger cleared his throat. "We found your husband's body at the old Rockford cabin. There were reports of gunfire. Sorry for your loss."

Brooke wiped wetness from her eyes. "This wasn't supposed to happen."

Trent kept an eye on Brooke. His blood pressure was a little low, but he insisted on walking out of the forest. He talked to the older ranger, then approached Brooke.

He put his hand on her shoulder. "How well did you know your neighbor?"

"Not well enough. He and his wife, and Nick and I, became friends when they moved into our neighborhood a year ago. His wife threw me a baby shower. I can't believe my eyes."

"Okay, little lady. Your blood pressure is low, and you're dehydrated. Let's get some fluids going, then we'll transport you and your miniature mountain man to the hospital. You could use a good meal, too."

"After the hospital, a shower and clean clothes are next on the list." Brooke stood and brushed at the back of her pants. Like it mattered. "Don't have to tell me twice."

Chapter Fifteen

Brooke held Josiah close to her chest and studied the team of men, who stepped forward with that basket thing Trent called a litter. She glanced at Trent and her rescuers. Her head spun, but only for a moment.

"Trent, would you carry Josiah?" He deserved the honor of carrying her baby out of the forest. His prized delivery. He remained true to his word. Admiration for his honesty, tenacity and integrity welled up. Desire to date him and see where the relationship went stirred her heart. They could discuss his work hours and come to an agreement. Peace washed over her.

Rex seemed to understand the question and gave a quick yelp.

A tiny hand escaped the cover of Mandy's blanket and reached for the sky. His little fingers formed into a fist, and he drew his hand to his face.

"Thought you'd never ask." Pure joy shown on Trent's face.

He looped Rex's leash around his hand and cradled her little bundle close to his chest. She'd never seen a grown man, so strong and masculine, hold his head so high. His attitude had shifted during their ordeal from a matter-of-fact, frustrated point of view to a more compassionate and appreciative demeanor. His kisses weren't so bad either. Warmth rushed to her cheeks at the thought.

"Let's get you settled. You've had a few rough days." The paramedic held her arm as she shuffled to the litter.

"You have no idea." She dropped her head. "It was a horrifying experience. I doubted surviving the forest until I stumbled into Trent's camp. He saved me and delivered my baby. I am truly blessed."

"Yes, ma'am. I don't believe in coincidences." He removed his cap, scraped fingers through his graying hair, and slid the cap back on. "The man upstairs looked out for you."

She lay back in the basket and they tossed straps over her and buckled her in. Her face reddened at the thought of body odor overpowering their sense of smell.

"Guess I don't have to tell you there weren't any showers out here." She curled her nose. "My apologies."

"No apology necessary. Glad to find all of you safe and sound." The redheaded man smiled. His gentle eyes comforted her concerns. "By the way, you smell like pine trees."

Trent and Rex followed behind several search and rescue men. Rangers tugged the killers up the incline a short distance away. Her baby's safety rested in confident hands.

"How far do we have to go?" The uphill trail ahead looked challenging. Beyond the pine trees, a small path met up with more rocks and protruding tree roots. She bounced in the litter with each step they took. The forest spun. A hand touched her arm.

"Hang with us. Your eyes are rolling," one man said. "Dehydration can do funky things. You're getting fluids and doing fine."

"Just beyond the ridge." The black-haired man spoke up. "Not far at all. We've got helicopters waiting to take you to the hospital. There's plenty of cold water and fruit to help sustain you until we land."

"Thank you." Emotions welled up. "I need to call my parents."

"Authorities have already notified them. They are expecting your arrival at the hospital."

Relief washed over her as her insides jumped for joy.

"They reported you missing three days ago, and Officer Williston's parents arrived at the ranger station two days ago and wouldn't go home. Not to mention a man and his son reported a pregnant woman on the trail, and we received a call by satellite phone about the shooting and your last known location."

Tears erupted. Rescue had finally arrived. Hikers were true to their word, too. She survived and would see her parents soon. A tsunami of tears flooded down her cheeks. Weakness crawled over her.

Brooke glanced back, but the team of rescuers blocked her view of the shelter Trent built with no tools. So many memories and uncertainties. A smile emerged when she spotted the white tail of a deer bouncing in the opposite direction.

Trent traipsed forward. Staunch and steady, with his brown-and-black canine trotting in front of him. Accepting Trent meant accepting Rex. She could handle the combo. Could they handle an instant family?

The whoop, whoop of a helicopter met with her ears as they emerged from the woods into an open meadow. Little yellow flowers decorated the field and danced in the wind. Her pursuers climbed into one helicopter with officials and the chopper lifted from the ground.

Trent waited with Josiah at the door of the other helicopter for the men to slide her inside. Rex sat at his feet with his back straight and his tail slapping the ground. The men boosted her inside, where a medic waited. Trent and Rex followed, along with two rangers. They passed out headsets to shield their ears from the noise and to talk to one another, as well as the pilot.

The senior ranger pulled out a small headset, apparently for children. He placed it over her baby's ears. It swallowed his little head, so they put small ear plugs in his miniature ears. It would have to do until they reached the helipad at the hospital.

The medic checked her blood pressure again and her temperature.

"I'm upping the drip on your IV fluids. You're severely dehydrated." He hung the fluid bag on a hook-like object inside the helicopter.

The chopper lifted, and her body became weightless. Her head spun and her eyes closed. She fought the odd sensations gripping her. She peeked at Trent, and her eyes rolled. Trent held her baby secure against his chest. She couldn't hold her eyes open, but voices came through her headset.

"She's out again." Trent said. "So exhausted. She's a real trouper. No one will ever believe what she's been through. Glad you guys found us when you did. No food, no water and no more strength. She even warmed up to Rex, I think."

"Doctors are on standby at the hospital. They'll know what to do." A deep-toned voice responded. "You're going to need fluids, too. You'll both be as good as new in a couple of days."

"ETA, twenty minutes." Must have been the pilot.

Her ears worked, but her body wouldn't. Dreams of a mattress, soft white sheets and a fluffy pillow drifted through her thoughts. She'd never take her amenities of home and city life for granted again. Hot coffee, iced tea and apple pie and ice cream.

Someone held her hand. She forced one eye open. Trent stared at her. The redness in his bloodshot eyes showed his weariness, too. His large hand swallowed hers. Warm and comforting. He raked his thumb across her knuckles.

She willed her hand to fold around his. Darkness took control.

"In here. Get another bag of ringers and start the antibiotic drip."

Brooke's eyes rolled open. Lights passed overhead. People stared down at her.

A familiar face appeared. Almost nose to nose. Mom, Beth, and Hannah stood behind her.

"Brooke, honey, you're safe now. We've been so worried." She wiped her nose with a tissue. "I just cannot imagine what you've been through. Your baby is beautiful. The doctor is checking him out now. I'll be right back. I'm going to see about him." A kiss hit her dirty cheek. "Love you. Your dad's here, too."

Oxygen found its way to her nostrils. "Breathe deep through your nose. You're doing fine." A red-headed nurse stood over her.

She blinked and widened her eyes. "What happened? Where's my baby?"

"You're safe. You're in the emergency room." Beth stood by her bed and held her hand. "I'm staying with you. Hannah went with mom and dad to see your baby."

"They said you passed out in the helicopter." The nurse checked her pulse. "Your baby is safe. The pediatrician is evaluating him, but from what I hear, he's a healthy little boy. They'll bring him back to you in a few minutes. Good job caring for him in the wild without all the amenities of home."

"Oh, you heard about that." She took a sip of ice water.

"Yes, and we're in awe of your bravery and incredible endurance." The nurse stood close and typed on the hospital computer.

"Thank you. I remember mom kissing me on the cheek." *It's over. Thank you, Lord.* "Where is Trent? He's the K-9 handler who delivered my baby."

Her nurse adjusted the IV. "He's in the next room receiving fluids, too. How the three of you survived four days without adequate food and water is beyond me."

"Trust me—it was all him. His knowledge of survival in the forest saved us and his police dog, Rex, alerted us to danger approaching. Trent delivered my baby and kept us alive. He risked his life for us." If only she could see him. She had only known him for a few days, and yet it seemed like they'd known each other for years. Only God could have brought them together and she wanted nothing else but for them to be just that. Together, always. This time, she trusted her instincts. Trent was the man for her.

A knock at her door interrupted her thoughts. Two Chattanooga Police officers stepped inside.

"Mrs. Chandler, I'm Officer Bates and this is Officer Hines. We're sorry about your situation, but we need to ask you a few questions. We found your husband's body." Bates flipped open a notepad and clicked his pen. "Can you tell us what happened?"

Brooke took in a deep breath. Reliving the total nightmare and sharing the details increased her heart rate and caused the heart monitor to beep. Her lip quivered and tears flowed as she recounted the entire story.

Beth squeezed her hand. "You did great, sis. Unbelievable."

The officers stared at her. Had they believed her wild story? Would they suspect her and separate her from Josiah? Her pulse increased even more. *Don't hyperventilate.*

"Thank you. We have the suspects in custody. May need you to testify in court." Officer Hines nodded. "Is there anything else you need to tell us before we go?"

"Only that Officer Trent Williston and his canine, Rex, risked their lives to protect me and my baby. I wouldn't have survived without them."

"They're a fine team and Trent is one of their best handlers." Officer Bates nodded and stopped at the door. "Thank you, and congratulations." He and the other officer left the room.

No doubts about Trent being one of the best. In her eyes, he *was* the best. She longed to see him and feel his closeness.

Trent guzzled water until one of his fellow officers brought him a large sweet iced tea and a loaded double cheeseburger with fries. Rex stayed outside with a fellow K-9 handler who brought food and water for him. Once they got home, Trent would give him a bath and brush and shine his fur.

They made it, and search and rescue showed up right on time. He pondered the entire ordeal and how his life and attitude had changed. The guilt and bitterness against God, and fear that had burrowed its way under his skin and tore at his heart after losing the preemie had diminished.

God answered his prayer when he delivered Josiah, and against all odds, the baby was healthy and perfect. He'd surrendered his brokenness and allowed God to heal his doubts. On top of it all, a beautiful angel made her way into his life in the most inconceivable way.

The doctor ordered more fluids for him, a CT scan on his head to make sure the bullet scrape didn't cause additional problems, and antibiotic cream for the bullet wound on his arm, then ordered an X-ray on his ankle. The technician rolled him back to his room.

"Good afternoon." The tall nurse lined up supplies on the rolling table. "I'm going to clean your wounds and bandage them."

"They're okay. I don't need anything."

She stared at him and lifted her eyebrows. "Doctor's

order to bandage those open wounds. What you do with the bandages after you leave is up to you."

"Whatever you say." *They'll be off before I walk out that door.* Where did they take Brooke? His fingers strummed the mattress. He had to see her.

"The X-ray on your ankle didn't show any signs of a fracture. I can wrap it, too."

"My ankle is fine. Seriously. Is that doctor's orders, too?"

"No. But I have a bandage if you want it." She shook her head. "I know. You don't want it." She finished with all the bandaging and closed the door behind her.

A light tapping drew him from his thoughts. The door to his room opened slowly and his mom stuck her head inside, then swung the door open wide. His parents and siblings flooded the room. Smiles and tears.

His brother, Todd, tossed a sack in his lap and set a super-large cup with a straw in it on his bedside table. The aroma of a burger and fries sent delightful shockwaves into his tastebuds. His brother didn't have to know a coworker had already delivered a burger.

"Sweet tea and a combo," his brother said. "Your favorite."

His mom dabbed the wetness from her face and scooped him into a mom hug. His dad shook his hand, then leaned down and patted his shoulder. His sister and brother repeated the actions of his parents.

"We were so worried when you didn't call or show up Sunday evening. We contacted the ranger's station. They said give you a little more time. The weather may have slowed your return, but I knew something wasn't right," his mom explained.

"I'm good, mom. No worries. Thank you for contacting authorities." Trent loved his family, but today he loved them even more. He looked at Dana. "Tell Mandy her baby blanket came in handy."

"You tell her." She held her phone out and dialed FaceTime.

"Uncle Trent." Her dainty voice warmed him. "You missed my party and my cake. You said you'd come. Where were you? Do you have my present?"

"Not yet, but I'll get it to you soon. Your baby blanket…"

"Okay. Bye." She hung up.

"She didn't give me a chance to tell her about the blanket." He handed the phone back.

"You can explain later. We heard you delivered a baby out there. I had no doubts you could pull it off." Dana patted his hand. "Never doubt your abilities. As mom always says, 'You can do anything you set your mind to.'"

"We want to hear all about it, but you can tell us over dinner." His dad sniffled. "Your mom is fixing one of your favorites, pot roast with all the fixings."

"I can hardly wait." Trent tossed another fry in his mouth and sucked in a big gulp of tea. "Depending on beef jerky and trail mix with a swallow of water isn't as great as it sounds. It kept us alive, though."

The nurse walked in and checked his IV. "Looks good. You've still got a little while to go."

His dad backed to the door. "I'm taking your mom home so she can get to cooking."

"The doctor said you'll be out of here as soon as you

get these fluids." His mom kissed his cheek. "See you soon. Love you."

"Love you, Mom, Dad." Trent watched them leave. His sister and brother stood staring at him. "What?"

"This pregnant woman just stumbled into your camp while running from killers?" His brother smirked. "Sounds like a horror movie."

"You have no idea." Trent emptied his tea.

"It will excite Mandy to know that you used her baby blanket to wrap around a real baby." Dana patted his hand. "Love you, brother. Now that I know you're safe, I've got to get back to work. See you at mom's tonight."

"I'm headed to the waiting room. Me and hospitals don't mix." His brother punched Trent's good arm. "They designated me your shuttle service. Oh, Dad dropped me off at the ranger's station to get your truck. Good thing you left an extra key on your dresser." He turned and walked away.

The nurse passed his open door.

"Nurse," he yelled.

"Yes."

"How is Brooke Chandler? She's the…"

"I know who she is, but I'll have to ask if she can have outside visitors, other than family." She started closing his door.

"But we were out there together. I need to know if she's okay." He held back his frustration.

The door closed. He fumed.

Trent slipped off the bed, still fully dressed, and un-hooked his saline bag from the IV pole. The yearning to have Brooke close grew stronger. After being side-by-side all that time and watching over her, he couldn't get her off his mind. Had she thought about him like he thought about her?

He held the bag up shoulder high and eased the door open. Only two people at the nurse's station and they had their backs to him. He'd heard Brooke's room was next to his, but which way? He slipped out and turned right. The closed window curtain made it impossible to peek inside, so he knocked on the door.

A gray-haired senior lady opened the door and an elderly balding man lay in the bed. Wrong room.

"My apologies. I have the wrong room." Trent looked around and froze when his nurse rounded the corner of the nurse's station. She disappeared into a little hall. He guessed into the area where doctors sit and put orders on the hospital computers.

He hugged the wall and slipped past his room. The curtain to the other room wasn't closed completely. He spotted Brooke lying on the bed. Two IVs going. A tall woman with hair like Brooke's stood beside her, brushing tangles out of Brooke's long brown hair. The pink scrunchie lay on the rolling table, along with a milk carton and a half-eaten sandwich.

He tapped on the door, noting the shaking in his hand. Weak? Nervous? His heart rate increased like a jackhammer. Would she be glad to see him, or did she want to forget the total nightmare and not want him around as a reminder?

The lady came to the door. Her eyes lit up. "Brooke, it's your protector. He's still making sure you're safe." She stepped aside. "Come in. I was just running to grab a soda. I'm Beth, by the way, her sister. You can stay with her." She eyed his IV bag. "Unless the nurse catches you and sends you back to bed."

Brooke's eyes brightened. "Are you supposed to be in here?"

"No." He walked closer to the side of her bed, still holding his fluid bag shoulder high. "How are you feeling? What's the doctor saying?" He placed his free hand on top of hers and squeezed.

"He said I'm doing a lot better than he expected. I have a slight infection, probably why I had fever, and I'm dehydrated, but we knew about dehydration. So, you're getting fluids, too."

"Yep. The nurse wouldn't tell me where you were. When she disappeared, I slipped out. Glad your sister is here. My parents and sister were here, but they left. My brother is in the waiting room. He doesn't care for hospitals. How's Josiah?"

"My parents are with him. The nurse is bringing him to me soon."

"That's good, really good." He cleared his throat and his mouth went dry. After all they'd been through, why was he suddenly nervous? "I needed to see you. Once you've had time to recover, would you and Josiah be interested in going to dinner sometime? I know how you feel about nature, so I won't force it on you, but Rex is a package deal."

Brooke turned her hand over and slid her fingers between his. "I've only known you four days, but I feel we've known each other for years. After our wild encounter, my attitude about the mountains has improved. I might consider returning sometime if I can stay in a nice cabin."

She hadn't answered his question. Maybe she wasn't interested.

His insides churned. Was that her way of putting him off?

"I'd love to spend more time with you. Bring Rex if you want, but you should know, Josiah and I are a package deal, too."

His chest swelled. "Gotta love a good bargain, especially when two come in the package." Trent licked his lips and swallowed. "And for the record, I talked to my sergeant and told him I needed to stick with regular work hours unless there's an emergency. After the eye-opening encounter I've had with you, I realize there's more to life than work and the preemie's death wasn't my fault. I've always wanted a family and you've made me realize the value of truth, love and time."

Her smile melted his heart.

She touched his arm. "The most important part is God protected and delivered us from the burdens that held us back. I'm elated at the thought of being with you."

He slipped his hand behind her head as he leaned and pressed his lips to hers.

* * * * *

LOVE INSPIRED

Stories to uplift and inspire

Fall in love with Love Inspired—
inspirational and uplifting stories of faith
and hope. Find strength and comfort in
the bonds of friendship and community.
Revel in the warmth of possibility and the
promise of new beginnings.

Sign up for the Love Inspired newsletter
at **LoveInspired.com** to be the first
to find out about upcoming titles,
special promotions and exclusive content.

CONNECT WITH US AT:

f Facebook.com/LoveInspiredBooks

t Twitter.com/LoveInspiredBks

LISOCIAL2021

Get 4 FREE REWARDS!

We'll send you 2 FREE Books plus 2 FREE Mystery Gifts.

FREE Value Over **$20**

Both the **Love Inspired®** and **Love Inspired® Suspense** series feature compelling novels filled with inspirational romance, faith, forgiveness, and hope.

YES! Please send me 2 FREE novels from the Love Inspired or Love Inspired Suspense series and my 2 FREE gifts (gifts are worth about $10 retail). After receiving them, if I don't wish to receive any more books, I can return the shipping statement marked "cancel." If I don't cancel, I will receive 6 brand-new Love Inspired Larger-Print books or Love Inspired Suspense Larger-Print books every month and be billed just $6.24 each in the U.S. or $6.49 each in Canada. That is a savings of at least 17% off the cover price. It's quite a bargain! Shipping and handling is just 50¢ per book in the U.S. and $1.25 per book in Canada.* I understand that accepting the 2 free books and gifts places me under no obligation to buy anything. I can always return a shipment and cancel at any time by calling the number below. The free books and gifts are mine to keep no matter what I decide.

Choose one: ☐ **Love Inspired**
Larger-Print
(122/322 IDN GRDF)

☐ **Love Inspired Suspense**
Larger-Print
(107/307 IDN GRDF)

Name (please print)

Address   Apt. #

City   State/Province   Zip/Postal Code

Email: Please check this box ☐ if you would like to receive newsletters and promotional emails from Harlequin Enterprises ULC and its affiliates. You can unsubscribe anytime.

Mail to the Harlequin Reader Service:
IN U.S.A.: P.O. Box 1341, Buffalo, NY 14240-8531
IN CANADA: P.O. Box 603, Fort Erie, Ontario L2A 5X3

Want to try 2 free books from another series! Call 1-800-873-8635 or visit www.ReaderService.com.

*Terms and prices subject to change without notice. Prices do not include sales taxes, which will be charged (if applicable) based on your state or country of residence. Canadian residents will be charged applicable taxes. Offer not valid in Quebec. This offer is, limited to one order per household. Books received may not be as shown. Not valid for current subscribers to the Love Inspired or Love Inspired Suspense series. All orders subject to approval. Credit or debit balances in a customer's account(s) may be offset by any other outstanding balance owed by or to the customer. Please allow 4 to 6 weeks for delivery. Offer available while quantities last.

LIRLIS22R2

HARLEQUIN
PLUS

Announcing a **BRAND-NEW**
multimedia subscription service
for romance fans like you!

Read, Watch and Play.

Experience the easiest way to get
the romance content you crave.

Start your **FREE 7 DAY TRIAL** at
<u>www.harlequinplus.com/freetrial</u>.

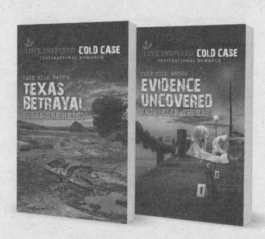
3 28 390